By Michael Butterworth

THE MAN WHO BROKE THE BANK AT MONTE CARLO
X MARKS THE SPOT
REMAINS TO BE SEEN
THE MAN IN THE SOPWITH CAMEL
VILLA ON THE SHORE
THE BLACK LOOK
FLOWERS FOR A DEAD WITCH
THE UNEASY SUN
THE SOUNDLESS SCREAM

The Man Who Broke the Bank at Monte Carlo

The Man Who Broke the Bank at Monte Carlo

MICHAEL BUTTERWORTH

PUBLISHED FOR THE CRIME CLUB BY
DOUBLEDAY & COMPANY, INC.
GARDEN CITY, NEW YORK
1983

All of the characters in this book are fictitious, and any resemblance to actual persons, living or dead, is purely coincidental.

Library of Congress Cataloging in Publication Data
Butterworth, Michael, 1924-
The man who broke the bank at Monte Carlo.
I. Title.
PR6052.U9M3 1983   823'.914
ISBN 0-385-18751-3
Library of Congress Catalog Card Number 82-48705
Copyright © 1983 by Michael Marlowe
All Rights Reserved
Printed in the United States of America
First Edition

*The Man Who Broke the Bank
at Monte Carlo*

CHAPTER 1

The Blue Train passed over the points at Calais Gare, causing the quail in aspic within the dining car to shudder delicately.

"Is the vichyssoise to your taste, Uncle Luigi?" asked Ernest Rowbotham of his companion, seated *vis-à-vis* in a wheelchair. The other did not vouchsafe an answer, but remained with his head slightly bowed, hands folded upon his lap. And, because he was wearing a broad-brimmed hat, not much could be seen of his face. He might even have been asleep. Or dead.

"As to the clientele in the dining car," said Rowbotham, "I checked the passenger list with the Head Steward and have, with his help, fitted faces to names.

"Seated immediately behind you is Mr. Diaghilev, Uncle, who, as you must know, is a Russian gentleman and the founder and director of the Diaghilev ballet, famous—among many others—for his production of *L'Après-midi d'un faune.*" Rowbotham was not very hot on French grammar and syntax, but he knew an accent when he saw one, and gave the fullthroat treatment to the second syllable of *après*.

"Accompanying Mr. Diaghilev is Mr. George Balanchine, who arranges ballets for the company. The other two gentlemen are Mr. Serge Lifar, dancer, and a Mr. Jean Cocteau, upon whom I have not been able to obtain any background information.

"Ah, here comes the second course. Waiter, my friend did

not much enjoy the vichyssoise, but I'm sure the vol-au-vent à la reine will suit him very well. Thank you so much.

"As I was saying, Uncle Luigi . . ."

As Ernest Rowbotham was saying, the First Class dining car (there was no other; the most distinguished train in the world, which carried the *jeunesse dorée* and the not so *jeunesse* to the Riviera—the Riviera, which might be said to have been invented by King Edward VII, Royal Voluptuary Extraordinary, and sanctified by all the Wealth, Beauty and Artistic Genius of the post-war generation—did not permit of anything but De Luxe) also included at least three vaudeville stars of the highest firmament, four millionaires, including Mr. Gordon Selfridge, the American Big Store entrepreneur, who was accompanied by the famous (giggling most of the time) Dolly sisters; a sprinkling of English and French aristocracy; a five-times-divorced Argentinian heiress and a Scottish laird who had accompanied the latter lady in to luncheon and was clearly doing his damnedest to become fancied favourite as husband number six at the starting line. All these Rowbotham described to his companion, the taciturn Uncle Luigi, who paid as little attention to the discourse as he paid to his vol-au-vent à la reine, as he had paid to his vichyssoise; but remained seated in his wheelchair, head slightly bowed, hands on lap.

And then, thought Ernest Rowbotham, there was the girl. Her name, as he had gleaned from the Head Steward, was Miss Annabel Smith and her passport described her as an "agent"—though an agent of what was not particularised. All in all, he decided that Uncle Luigi would not be greatly interested in Miss Smith, agent; though it could be said that the lady in question (she was about thirty years of age in Rowbotham's judgement of womankind, which was not considerable; statuesquely built, dark hair drawn back in round plaits over each ear—like the earphones of a wireless receiver

—and steel-rimmed spectacles) appeared to be taking more than a passing interest in them: she seemed to cock an ear every time Rowbotham addressed his companion, and every so often made some jottings in a notebook which she had open beside her plate. Rowbotham, who had a capacity for characterising people—which he always attributed to half a lifetime as a schoolmaster—put her down as a lady novelist in quest of "background"—but, if a lady novelist, surely one who had attained a considerable success, to be travelling on the Blue Train.

Having given his uncle a brief survey of their present companions, Rowbotham addressed himself to his braised sweetbreads financière, which, in the event, he never finished.

It was only a mile or so further on, at a wayside station just clear of Calais, that the Blue Train came to a sudden, juddering halt, so that the Very Reverend Dean of Midchester Cathedral nearly swallowed his false teeth along with a mouthful of York ham, and the Dolly sisters screamed and clung to Mr. Gordon Selfridge.

"What the hell is going on, fellow?" Given an emergency of this sort, there is always an Englishman—usually of the naval or military persuasion—who can be relied upon to "take charge"; there was indeed one of that sort in the dining car who rose to the occasion, and he addressed his demand to the Head Steward, who, after having gone forward to find out what was amiss, presently returned, ashen-faced.

"Well, out with it, man!" barked the Englishman, who, from his full beard, was clearly of the naval persuasion. "I've been travelling on this damned train for ten years, and we've never had need to stop at this damned out-of-the-way hole before. What goes on, hey?"

"Monsieur," replied the unhappy functionary, and, extending his address to the remainder of the dining car, "Milords and miladies, mesdames et messieurs, the train 'as been stopped by the police, who are seeking an escaped murderer, and it is thought that he may 'ave boarded le Train Bleu at Calais."

"A murderer! Gordon, darling, are we in any *peril?*" This from one of the Dolly sisters.

"Nothing to worry your pretty head about, dear," said the tycoon.

"*Quel drame!*" ejaculated Diaghilev. "I tell you, Jean, that I would not be elsewhere for ten thousand francs. *Quel frisson!*"

"Uncle Luigi, there appears to be some kind of trouble," said Rowbotham dutifully, "but I don't think we need concern ourselves."

The police entered the dining saloon. They comprised a burly man in a check suit and derby hat, accompanied by two *agents* in kepis and capes.

"Mesdames et messieurs!" announced the leader of the posse, immediately breaking off into English when he discerned the make-up of the clientele. "My assistants and I will pass among you and make certain enquiries which will take a few minutes, no more. Continue with your *déjeuner*. *Bon appétit.*"

"They're going to quiz us, Uncle," murmured Rowbotham. "And I hope to God they don't rumble you."

Uncle Luigi made no response.

The police were most certainly swift and civil in their endeavours. After all, what does a lowly, underpaid and overworked cop do when confronted by a French marquis of the *ancien régime,* a *noble d'épée,* whose heraldic quarterings include the arms of half the principal noble families of Europe, whose face is known to all, with an ancestor who died in the arms of St. Louis on a Crusade (so very, very many ancestors are reputed to have died in the arms of St. Louis it is a wonder that that saintly monarch ever had time to fight a Crusade); and how does he deal with the Dean of Midchester, not to speak of a five-times-married Argentinian heiress, the Dolly sisters—and Mr. Gordon Selfridge?

The examination of the distinguished passengers in the dining car of the Blue Train, let it be said, was perfunctory and exiguous to an almost laughable degree.

Until they came to Ernest Rowbotham—and his Uncle Luigi.

"Your passports, messieurs."

"I have a British passport," said Rowbotham, "but my friend, that's to say my uncle, does not require one."

Much eyebrow raising. A distinct sense of hidden revolvers being loosened in holsters. The man in the derby hat cast a sharp glance at the figure in the wheelchair, who had not moved all this time, but still remained seated with hands serenely folded on lap, head bowed, silent.

"Your friend, your—as you say—uncle, he is a British citizen, monsieur?" The question had a very hard edge on it.

"Er—lately American citizen, formerly Italian," said Rowbotham.

The detective let a little time go by, breathed heavily a few times and returned to the attack. "Does this lately American citizen not possess an American passport?" he asked, with considerable restraint. "Or does not this formerly Italian citizen possess a passport from the source of his origin—if that is the correct expression? I am being very patient with you, monsieur, which you must concede."

"My Uncle Luigi has neither an American passport nor an Italian," declared Rowbotham. "And he is in no need of either"—he took a deep breath—"considering his condition."

The detective stared at Uncle Luigi, who had not stirred throughout the dialogue. And every eye, every ear, in the dining car was directed towards them; even the kitchen staff had crowded into the gangway, tall white hats and all, and were gawping, open-mouthed, to hear and see the outcome.

"Why does Monsieur not need a passport?" demanded the detective. "And why does he not speak for himself? Is he, perhaps, a deaf mute?"

"He's in very much worse state than that," said Ernest Rowbotham, knowing that he had, so to speak, got to the end of the line.

The detective then gave a brusque gesture, contingent upon which one of his aides whipped off the broad-brimmed hat of the figure in the chair. With it, also, came a light mask of silk, flesh-coloured, that had entirely covered the face.

In the aghast silence that followed this unveiling, one of the Dolly sisters slipped slowly and with practised elegance to the richly carpeted floor; her sibling, not wishing to be upstaged, then followed her.

"He's dead, you see," explained Rowbotham—an understatement if there ever was one, for his Uncle Luigi was not only discernibly defunct, but had clearly departed this Vale of Tears at some remove in time. Furthermore, he had not only been embalmed or mummified, but with complete disregard for the aesthetics of the craft. Uncle Luigi was a fright.

"So it appears, monsieur," murmured the detective.

"But, although he looks pretty awful," said Rowbotham, "he's quite sanitary and all that, not doing anyone any harm. And it's perfectly legal in France to transport a properly embalmed corpse by public conveyances. We enquired upon this point, or at least"—indicating Uncle Luigi—"*he* did."

If the detective had survived the sudden encounter with the mummified Uncle Luigi, the same could not be said for most of the folk in the compartment. In addition to the Dolly sisters—both being ministered to by Mr. Gordon Selfridge, who was on the knees of his dove grey pants beside them with soft words, cheek and hand patting, sal volatile—the younger of the two *agents* had so far succumbed to the shock that he felt constrained, and indeed was encouraged, to take the vacant seat beside Mr. Diaghilev, who then proceeded to dispense a similar treatment to the ashen-faced youth.

"Monsieur—er—Rowbotham," said the detective, "I suggest that we retire to the privacy of your compartment and discuss this matter. All—er—three of us."

"Of course," said Rowbotham, and replacing the silk mask and the broad-brimmed hat upon Uncle Luigi, he steered the wheelchair out of the dining car; concerted gusts of exhaled breath and sighs of relief followed them.

"My dear Jenny, my dear Rosie, are you all right?" purred Gordon Selfridge, helping Miss Jenny to her feet and savagely striking away the arm of a waiter who had the temerity similarly to assist Miss Rosie.

"It was awful—*awful!*" declared Miss Jenny. "I shall never be able to face vol-au-vent à la reine again!"

"And the way its mouth was *stitched up!*" cried her sister. "Just like a patch on an old pair of pants!"

"Girls, girls, forget it," advised the great tycoon. "Tomorrow night, in recompense, I will stake you to play in the *salles privées* for the maximum."

"Darling Gordon, you are so good to us," said the sisters more or less in unison. "What have we done to deserve your kindness?"

"*Arriviste!*" murmured the French marquis with the quarterings that went back to the First Crusade. He looked away from Selfridge in distaste, slackened the great muscle surrounding his eye and allowed his monocle to fall and dangle on the end of its black moiré ribbon.

The Englishman of the naval persuasion had as his table companion a handsome widow from Boston, Massachusetts, whose fortitude in the face of Uncle Luigi's sewn-up, rictus grin had been considerably propped up by the other's aplomb;

she declared, "My, Admiral, you certainly didn't let that awful bogeyman scare you. My husband, the late Colonel Willibrand, was a man of a like calibre."

"Ma'am," responded the admiral, leaning forward and taking both of her plump, heavily beringed hands in his gnarled, bronzed fingers, "we are in foreign parts. When one has served in all corners of our far-flung Empire, as I have, and one has seen foreign parts, one comes to realize that in the latter places, the unexpected is normal, the bizarre commonplace, the grotesque purely routine. Will you dine with me in Monte Carlo tomorrow, Mrs. Willibrand?"

Normalcy was returning to the dining car: the Head Steward had shooed the kitchen staff back to their duties; some of the clientele were even essaying to tackle their food again, or at least to push it unenthusiastically about their plates.

"A cognac will be of advantage to you, officer," said Diaghilev, addressing the young policeman, who was looking decidedly more wholesome than he had been a few minutes before. "You interest me. Such strong hands. Such artistic fingers."

Forward, in the De Luxe sleeping compartment that he shared with Uncle Luigi, poor Ernest Rowbotham was being closely interrogated by the detective as to why and how he was in possession of a corpse of dubious provenance, and transporting the same aboard the most prestigious train in the world, and for what reason.

Meanwhile, the Blue Train sped on its way through the fair fields of northern France, while the diligent *agents de police* continued the search for the missing murderer—who, indeed, was found hiding in the baggage compartment. This wretch, who had killed his own mother in order to steal her money and pay an *apache* to murder the ponce who had put his girl friend on the streets, had been on his way under escort to Paris to be guillotined. He was taken from the baggage compartment and placed in an empty De Luxe sleeper in charge of two policemen; so his escape had provided, fortuitously, a quite considerable advantage for him on his final journey.

The news of the recapture, when it was brought to the passengers in the dining car, caused another *frisson* of vicarious excitement, which soon faded as the effects of a heavy luncheon washed down with fine wines and spirits took their toll in ennui.

Diaghilev put it rather well: "The excitement is all over. How mundane things seem now. I am bored. Astonish me, Jean."

Meanwhile, having satisfied the detective to some degree and seen him depart, Ernest Rowbotham sat down on his bunk, buried his face in his hands and had an onset of despair, which was not lightened by the presence of the hunched, hatted, masked figure in the wheelchair opposite him.

He looked up.

"Why the bloody hell did I let myself get stuck with *you?*" he cried.

CHAPTER 2

The chain of events that led to Ernest Rowbotham being aboard the Blue Train with a badly stuffed corpse began with the circumstances of his birth. His father, an entrepreneur and importer of fancy goods, met and married—while searching southern Italy for handmade local pottery and glassware to buy cheaply and sell dear in London, Manchester and Birmingham—a Signorina Francesca Gaudi, formerly of Palermo, Sicily. The couple eventually settled down in Worthing, Sussex and produced a child, Ernest. Rowbotham *père*, his wandering ways tamed by the strong will of a good woman, gave up his commercial travelling, opened a fancy goods emporium on the Worthing sea front and prospered mightily—till the First World War came along. One day in 1914, having imbibed rather heavily with his fellow members of the Ancient Order of Bisons, he persuaded himself to enlist in the Royal Sussex Yeomanry as a private soldier, and was killed—along with twenty thousand others of his sort—one Saturday morning on the Somme, for the purpose of taking a couple of hundred yards of German trenches, which were lost that same afternoon.

Francesca Rowbotham grieved her husband day and night for a week, totally unconsolable by anyone, even her son, who was in the middle of his finals at Cambridge, but who came down to be with his bereaved mother. At the end of the week, Mrs. Rowbotham dried her eyes, sent Ernest packing up to Cambridge with a flea in his ear and went back to running the emporium, which, it has to be said, she had been doing with infinitely more style and efficiency than her late husband while he had been away at the Front.

Ernest graduated with a good second-class degree and no idea about what he was going to do. The Great War ended and he was saved from the holocaust by an accidental combination of age, the furtherance of an approved university course and a tendency to asthma which alone would have kept him out of the trenches if not out of the Army. Ernest found himself at the tail end of the queue for jobs that were being clamoured for by discharged servicemen returning to Mr. Lloyd George's Country Fit for Heroes to Live In. He had no taste for shopkeeping, nor would his mother have permitted him to work in the emporium: with her peasant shrewdness, she argued that one does not pay out for a lad to go through university for four years in order to come back and sell Benares brassware and reproduction Tuscan urns to holiday-makers from the Midlands. Ernest had been educated for a Profession, and a professional job he must get. Six months later, Mrs. Rowbotham died suddenly of a cerebral haemorrhage.

Still with no job, and completely distraught, Ernest had no recourse (since, as he was aware, he had neither the ability nor the inclination to do it himself) but to repose the running of the emporium to the capable hands of one Jesse Ogden, a young man of his own age who had been called up in the Army but had contrived to get no nearer to the firing line than standing guard on Brighton sea front. Ogden was a hard worker, and ambitious. Under the late Mrs. Rowbotham's sharp eye and tutelage, his capacity for hard work had been thoroughly exploited and his ambition kept within bounds. He rejoiced at the opportunity to manage the business—and told his benefactor so in unequivocal terms. Ernest Rowbotham was much relieved, shook the other by the hand, wished him luck—and went back to looking for a professional job, safe in the knowledge that he was, at least, secure—with between £60 and £80 a month being paid into his bank account from the profits of the business. It was shortly after this arrangement was made that he managed to land himself into that profession which is the last resort and repository of the educated: schoolmastering.

The Hillbrough Hall College for the Sons of Christian Gentlemen was almost what it claimed to be. Situated in the picturesque Peak District of Derbyshire, a rambling Victorian mansion in the semi-classical style, it catered for dullards of from fourteen upwards who, having been unable to pass the Common Entrance Examination that admits sons of gentlemen into more prestigious Groves of Academe, and with not a hope in hell of matriculating, needed to be kept in check till they were of an age to turn loose upon the world outside.

The establishment was the brain-child of, and run by, the Reverend Mr. Thomas T. Thorseby, M.A. (Oxon), a divine of some sixty summers, married to a very capable woman twenty years younger than himself, and possessing a nubile and extremely pretty virgin daughter named Felicity, aged seventeen. The Thorsebys lived in the former dower house of the former minor stately home, a quarter of a mile from the college buildings and surrounded by a *cordon sanitaire* of a high fence, an injunction that no boys were permitted to approach within fifty yards of the same without a pass signed by Matron—the whole enforced by the roaming presence of an Alsatian dog, who, in the folklore of the pupils, passed down by word of mouth, was kept in a perpetual state of semi-starvation only occasionally enlivened by being fed pieces of small boys of the lower classes whom Tom Tit (their nickname for the Reverend Thorseby) lured in from the highways and byways at dead of night. By such contrivances did the headmaster of Hillbrough Hall College seek to preserve the virginity of his lovely young daughter from the forty-odd youths, all boarders, who were his pupils—and at most astronomical fees.

He need scarcely have bothered. The regimen of the establishment, which he had devised in collaboration with his capable wife, would have driven thoughts of carnality from Casanova himself.

The routine, which Ernest Rowbotham and the other two assistant masters had to partake of also, was as follows:

    5:45—Rise.   12:00—Prayers.
    6:00—Two mile run.   12:30—Luncheon.
    7:00—Cold Bath.   1:00—Organised games.
    7:30—Prayers.   4:00—Tea.
    8:00—Breakfast.   4:30—Prayers.
    8:30—Lessons.   5:00—Rest Period.*
  10:00—Gymnasium.   5:30—Housekeeping.†
  10:30—Lessons.   6:30—Lessons.

        8:00—Supper.
        8:30—Prayers.
        9:00—Write letters home (Sundays only).
        9:30—Bed. Lights out.

The diet of cold baths, prayer and physical activity certainly damped the rumbustious spirits of the boys (this was also aided by adding bromide to their supper cocoa—another of Mrs. Thorseby's bright ideas), but it had the curious effect of sharpening Rowbotham's carnal desires and, indeed, im-

---

* The half-hour Rest Period was withdrawn, for the whole term, upon the lightest infringement of the Rules of the College, and the offender put on to Extra Housekeeping (q.v.).

† Devised by Mrs. Thorseby, after the manner of the Squeerses of Dotheboys Hall in *Nicholas Nickleby*, whereby pupils learned practical things like painting and decorating, washing dishes, scrubbing floors, by actually *doing* them.

proving his health. A year after joining the college he had put on weight, given up cigarettes, suffered scarcely at all from attacks of asthma—and conceived a passion for that empaled beauty, the now eighteen-year-old and visibly burgeoning virgin Felicity. While the boys of Hillbrough Hall lay in their chaste dormitory beds, their heated passions cooled, their rising sap held in check by cold baths, prayer, exercise and bromide, Rowbotham would fret restlessly in his attic room, tossing from side to side, sleepless; craving to lay his hand upon Felicity's, to kiss her peach-like cheek, even—and the thought left him breathless—to insinuate his importuning fingers into her well-filled bodice.

It happened on his second Christmas at the college, when he was invited, along with the other junior masters, to partake of a glass of temperance beverage at the dower house after Second Chapel on Christmas Day. They presented themselves, the three of them, at the front door, having passed through the gate of the high fence and skirted the slavering fangs of the Alsatian (chained up for the Festive Occasion), were received by the Reverend and Mrs. Thorseby and taken to the drawing-room, which was full of overstuffed Victorian furniture, religious paintings and prints whose subject matters mirrored the Thorsebys' essentially Fundamentalist leanings, and —to Rowbotham's instant and intense delight—Felicity Thorseby in a long frock, her hair gathered in a chignon, her baby blue eyes modestly lowered, her adorable bosom rising and falling in the excitement of being confronted by three lustful young animals of the opposite sex.

The empaled maiden had been brought forth. She, whom Rowbotham and the others had only seen across the width of the college chapel at Sunday mattins, or from afar when she was driven out by her father and mother in their Model-T

Ford, was with them. Among them. Could be spoken to. Listened to.

Touched . . .

The contrivance by which Rowbotham managed to be alone with Felicity Thorseby was entirely fortuitous, and not of his own devising, but, on reflection, he often wondered if she had not played a part in it. The headmaster and the other two assistants shared an interest in archaeology in which Rowbotham did not join. They went to the Reverend Thorseby's study to view some interesting palaeolithic fossils. And that left Rowbotham alone with the two females.

What happened next remained in his mind like an ever-shifting magic-lantern slide. Upon some suggestion from Felicity that the Christmas turkey might be burning, her mother fled to the kitchen.

They were alone. She was sitting on the well-stuffed sofa, hands folded demurely on her lap, cheeks flaming. A long time went past.

Presently, he said, "I like your frock."

"I made it myself," she replied.

Already, he could hear the voices of his employer and colleagues as they descended the staircase from the Reverend's study. It was an even bet—considering the stratagems the Thorsebys got up to to shield their daughter from the world of Menfolk—that the mother would hurry from the kitchen and arrive back at the drawing-room door neck and neck with her spouse.

It was now or never! Seating himself beside the object of his passion, Rowbotham put one arm about her waist, drawing her to him, and kissed her full upon the lips. Her moist mouth fell open in a gasp and he felt the warmth within her. Next, with the Reverend Thorseby's booming bray dinning in his ears from the bottom of the staircase outside the door, he lightly cupped her left bosom—over the material—and gave it a slight squeeze. They were sitting well apart, and both breathing heavily, when the others entered. One more glass of temperance beverage, and the festivities were over.

The next morning, Ernest Rowbotham received a peremptory note advising him of the time of the train that he must catch. He was dismissed summarily, and without a reference.

What had happened was this: in the dark hours of the night, that empaled child of Ignorance, Felicity, after battling long with her conscience and her terror of her parents, had gone to their room and made her confession:

She had allowed Ernest Rowbotham to "interfere with her" —and now she must surely be going to have his baby!

Worthing had no charm for him, only memories of his relatively happy childhood and the recollection of his orphaned state. He rented a bed-sitting-room in Pimlico, London, and enrolled with a couple more scholastic agencies, who, divining that the circumstances of his departure from Hillbrough Hall had been less than propitious, pulled long lips and said that the profession was greatly overcrowded, but keep in touch.

A couple of months after getting the sack, he received a letter from the manager of the bank in Worthing where he kept his account, informing him that he was £350.11.6 overdrawn, and would he please take immediate steps to adjust the matter? Yours faithfully, etcetera, etcetera.

Rowbotham was down to Worthing by the next train and bearding Jesse Ogden in the emporium, where the latter suavely explained that, yes, he had been remiss in informing his employer that he had been unable to credit his account with the usual monthly funds. And the reason he had not been able to bank the same was due to seasonal fluctuation of trade—which was certain to pick up just as soon as the holiday season started at Easter. And by a happy chance, added Ogden, there was around £400 of cash in the safe, so Mr. Rowbotham would be able to adjust his account right away. Which Rowbotham did. He then returned to London, somewhat chastened by the knowledge that he would greatly have to curtail his style of living till trade picked up with the beginning of the holiday-making season and folks started to flock down to the south coast with well-stuffed wallets and hands eager to lay themselves upon Benares brassware and reproduction Tuscan urns. It really wouldn't be too bad, he told himself. One could manage quite nicely on, say, £3 a week, and Ogden had smilingly assured him that the profits of the shop, after overheads, would certainly cover his expenditure of £3 a week indefinitely.

Alas for assurances . . .

The following week, Jesse Ogden absconded to South America with all the liquidity of the business, which he had systematically been juicing away ever since he took over. With him, as comforter, he took a chorus girl from the Worthing Pier Pavilion production of *Chu Chin Chow*. The Official Receiver, when Rowbotham was obliged to go bankrupt, estimated that Ogden must have amassed around £30,000. The entire stock was not paid for. By some arcane means, he had managed to raise bank loans and mortgages on the property (which was only rented anyhow). All he had missed, all that had slipped through his sticky fingers, was the £400 cash which he had given Rowbotham to keep him quiet for a few days. And that, thought Rowbotham wryly, must have hurt him a lot.

There followed the most wretched years of his life, when, totally without the support of his patrimony, he was obliged to accept the most degrading of jobs in the scholastic profession—but always in the memory of his mother, he remained within the professional orbit. There was a school in North Yorkshire, run by a sadist with degrees from Edinburgh and

Heidelberg, which was an expensive dumping-ground for the unwanted boys of the very rich, and which differed from Hillbrough Hall only in matters of detail: flogging was substituted for prayer as a specific for taming the inner beast in a boy; sickened by the sight of so many lacerated buttocks during communal bath-time, Rowbotham quit within a term. His last affray with the then deplorable private school *mélange* came when he took up an appointment as Games Master at an establishment in West Suffolk, which, because of its propinquity to Newmarket racecourse, was a hell-hole of gambling. The headmaster, himself born into horse-racing and the son of a Newmarket trainer, would bet on anything, even on what the next chap who came into the pub would order, or on the colour of the barmaid's knickers. Timidly and ineptly supervising the boys at their games of cricket and Rugby football, Rowbotham was always aware that, on race days, various members of the teams were being deputed by their fellows to drift away and place bets with the local bookie. He grew to accept that it was useless to punish, probably fruitless to complain to the headmaster, for whom the very same boys were almost certainly laying bets also. The end came when the headmaster assembled every penny he could lay hands on—this included the current and deposit accounts of the school, the Consolidation Fund, the Advance Fees Fund, the masters' and domestic staffs' salaries and wages for the month ahead, his own fortune and that of his wife—and placed the whole lot on a filly running in the Caesarewich called Titty-Fallah, which, by his own judgement following a lifetime of following form, could not possibly lose, albeit that the bookies were giving her ten to one. Titty-Fallah ran a good race and came home fifth out of a field of seventeen, whereupon the headmaster, without repining, took his wife's very pretty Suffolk country girl housemaid to bed and pleasured her greatly, then drank half a bottle of fine malt whisky, put his old service revolver in his mouth and blew the top of his head off. Ernest Rowbotham was unemployed again.

It was then, in the form of the kind of Good Fairy that so often illuminates the pages of literature but is infrequently encountered in real life, he received a letter from a firm of international lawyers. The postmark was London, but the firm, from the letterhead, was centered in Chicago, Illinois. The letter concluded with a classic sentence:

"*If you will communicate with us, you will learn something to your advantage.*"

Rowbotham had dim recollections of his mother's family. There was an Aunt Angelina who came over from Sicily to visit them shortly after the war. This was both the first time he had heard his mother gabble away in an incomprehensible language and the first time that she, who had totally and conscientiously Anglicised herself upon marrying the personable commercial traveller, had served Italian food at the family table. Aunt Angelina did not speak English, and the sisters' conversation was almost entirely incomprehensible to him—save for the constantly recurring proper name Luigi, a name that was pronounced by the pair of them in the same sort of hushed tones of deep respect that Englishmen reserve for, say, Lord Nelson, or Americans for Thomas Jefferson.

Their brother Luigi, his mother explained to him, had literally immigrated to America as a barefoot boy with his worldly possessions tied up in the traditional spotted handkerchief, and had made good in Chicago. Indeed, had made very good, to the extent that he had been able to provide their mother with the finest mausoleum in San Salvatore, Palermo, and was putting Aunt Angelina's two boys through Palma university. The extent of Uncle Luigi's benefactions to the family were legion, for he appeared to possess unlimited wealth and influence, not only in Chicago, but also, at some remove, in Sicily. It was never specified, nor did Mrs. Rowbotham ever allude to, the precise nature of Uncle Luigi's occupation in the Windy City on Lake Michigan.

At the offices of the lawyers Platts, Brinkley, Hobbs, Hobbs and Bailey, to which Rowbotham speedily repaired upon their summons, he learned to his astonishment that, Uncle Luigi having died, he had been named as sole heir to the deceased man's very considerable fortune, estimated at around six million dollars. To allow him to recover from the shock, they gave him a cup of coffee in a quiet room and left him alone with a sealed envelope. This, they told him, contained the conditions upon which he was to receive the bequest. Take your time, they said. No hurry. No hurry at all.

Ernest Rowbotham drank his coffee and gazed at the envelope lying on the table beside him, regarding it with the fascination of a rabbit confronting a stoat. Twice he extended his hand to take it up, twice he withdrew.

It was a hoax. That much he decided. Uncle Luigi's name had never passed his mother's lips save the time that Aunt Angelina had come to stay just after the war; this was possibly accounted for by her deliberate policy of self-Anglicisation. If she had so far cut herself off from her family (the visit of Aunt Angelina excepted), how had Uncle Luigi even come to hear of him, let alone decide to make him his sole heir?

The letter, of course, would give the answer; he took it up and opened it. The contents were neatly typed as by a competent secretary on expensive, deckle-edged notepaper—and only defaced by the signature at the foot, which looked, in the felicitous phrase of Mr. Andrew Barton ("Banjo") Patterson, that renowned Australian balladeer, as if it had been "written with a thumbnail dipped in tar."

Chicago, Illinois.
November 18

Dear Nephew Ernest,
My sister Angelina, when she was over here this fall, has told me of you. Your mother I never forgave for wedding a Limey, but now that my time is coming I want to bury old grudges. My sister your Aunt Angelina tells me you're a pretty nice guy who's been educated at the Cambridge College, England, and this suits me fine since I guess you've been around some and seen places and done things.

Ernest, since I was 18 and came to the States on my own, all I ever did was hustle. Sometimes I'd tell myself, "Luigi, one day you're going to Europe and spend all that money on doing all the things you've dreamed of." It never happened. By the time you read this I will be ordering drinks from that Great Bartender in the Sky. But my heart will be back down there, with all the places I never went to, the dreams I dreamed that never came true.

Around New Year, when I'm dead, there's a mortician in Greener Street who's going to fix what's left of me so you wouldn't know the difference. I've been stuck in a wheelchair since the time when I had a slight accident, so a wheelchair is no stranger to me.

Ernest, what I ask of you is this, that you take what's left of me in that goddamned wheelchair to all the places that I should have made if I hadn't been so goddamned crazy on hustling the bucks. If you want the job, the money, all of it, is yours. If you don't, it goes to the Universal Dogs' Home of Cincinnati, which institution has always been my favourite charity on account of I consider dogs in general to be more trustworthy than persons.

I hope you'll accept the deal, Ernest. In which case we will have a lot of laughs together. You in the flesh, me in the spirit.

Looking forward to meeting you.

Yours ever,

Uncle Luigi

P.S. Attached to this letter is a schedule of the places I want you to take me in the wheelchair, the kind of duds I want you to fit me out with, the kind of high society folks I want you to introduce me to. With your kind of background we don't have any problems in these respects.

P.P.S. Funniest thing. You know, I'm really looking forward to New Year and that journey I never made.

For reasons he could not have analysed to save his life, Ernest Rowbotham's eyes were hazed with tears by the time he had read the missive and perused the schedule attached thereto.

The first item in the schedule ran: *Take the Blue Train down to Monte Carlo and check in at Le Paris Hotel.*

And then: *Immediately upon arrival, take from my baggage the heart-shaped lead casket and deposit it in the hotel safe.*

Which was why Ernest and his Uncle Luigi were where they were—and it was a pity that the whole thing had got off to such a disastrous start.

CHAPTER 3

Though, thanks to a guarded upbringing and a natural tendency to shyness, Ernest Rowbotham could not have been described as a Man of the World, he was, nevertheless, well educated and quite shrewd after his fashion. Immediately upon receiving the news from Messrs. Platts, Brinkley, Hobbs, Hobbs and Bailey (and incidentally indicating to them that he accepted the terms of the bequest), he set about to learn something of his departed Uncle Luigi; this he did by spending a day at the British Museum Reading Room and another at the London Library, from whence he followed an ever-opening trail through various news agencies and clipping agencies. By the end of the week, what had begun as no more than a hunch had hardened into a certainty: Uncle Luigi had made his fortune as a Chicago bootlegger and gang boss.

The ramifications of his uncle's "business" were too arcane, too convoluted, to make a straight narrative in any source of reference that Rowbotham consulted, but he managed to assemble a skeletal *curriculum vitae* from fragments of news here and there, agency photos and even a certain amount of ill-informed hearsay picked up in Fleet Street pubs.

Uncle Luigi had been a big-time gang boss of the second magnitude. No Capone, he, no Touhy, Dion O'Banion, Frank Costello or even Ralph Sheldon. Uncle Luigi had held his own in warring Chicago by being Mr. Good Guy, the friend of all the big shots, the honest broker when it came to patching up bloody disagreements about territories, the lead to all the malleable politicians in the State Capitol and at City Hall. In return for these various favours, Luigi Gaudi had won himself a lot of goodwill right across the board. When O'Banion was not speaking to Capone—which was often—the two of them nevertheless were on good terms with Luigi, the Nice Guy. For his services rendered, he was granted full rights on what was hard O'Banion territory: a couple of prestigious blocks between Ashland and Western; likewise Capone gave him feudal fiefdom of a long piece of West Fifty-fifth Street, bordering on the fiefdom of the Saltis Gang. In both these areas, Luigi Gaudi greatly prospered. Sticking strictly to beer and whisky (prostitution, as a nicely brought-up Catholic boy, he eschewed; though, as events were to prove, he later had carnal thoughts in this direction), he built up a solid business compounded of good stuff regularly delivered at attractive prices—added to a thoroughly ruthless method of collecting payment from bilkers: at least a quarter of the unsolved killings attributed to O'Banion, Capone and Saltis could be laid at Luigi Gaudi's door.

And then fate frowned upon the honest broker. Mr. Good Guy, the Fixer, put a foot wrong. One of his boys had a fight in a bar with a member of another gang in which the latter was taken to hospital with a fractured skull from which he presently shrugged off this mortal coil. With the inexorable code of the Chicago mobster, the rival mob next day gunned down one of Gaudi's lieutenants as he was emerging from Mass. There the matter should have rested, on the excellent principle of an Eye for an Eye, a Tooth for a Tooth. For once, however, the Fixer got it wrong; instead of closing the account there and then as even, he irritably ordered a retaliation: no less than the leader of the other gang was taken for a ride and his ears sent to his widow through the mail with a scurrilous four-line doggerel. The next day, Uncle Luigi was shot in the back while taking luncheon at his favourite restaurant, contingent upon which he became a paraplegic, condemned forever to a wheelchair.

The details of all this here recorded were, of course, only known to Rowbotham in very general terms, together with the information that Uncle Luigi had contracted cancer of the spleen some six months previously and had died, strictly in accordance with the prognosis which he had demanded, within a couple of days into the New Year.

The Blue Train passed through Cannes, Juan-les-Pins, Cagnes-sur-Mer and across the estuary of the river Var into Nice. At Nice, many of the passengers, including the Diaghilev *ensemble,* the French marquis, the British admiral and his putative *amie* the widow from Boston, Massachusetts, and many others alighted. The point being that the Blue Train ceased, after Cannes, to be an express and traipsed in and out of every wayside station along the Côte D'Azur. The very rich detrained at Nice, where they were met by their chauffeurs and their Rolls-Royces, their Bugattis, Mercedes-Benzes, Isotta-Frashcinis, Hispano-Suizas, Daimlers and so forth, to be taken to their palm-and-bougainvillaea-girt villas overlooking the breath-taking blueness of the bay. Rowbotham and Uncle Luigi departed with the nobs, and were greeted by a chauffeur in a pale violet uniform and cap, with shiny jackboots (these details of costume had been specifically specified in Uncle's schedule), together with a Duesenberg with French-styled sedanca de ville bodywork (also scheduled, and hideously difficult to obtain; Rowbotham had spent a fortune in wires and long-distance phone calls to secure it). The chauffeur, who was French, spoke excellent English and presented himself as Charles; did not bat an eyelid when commanded to lift Uncle Luigi from his wheelchair, place him in the back of the limousine and stow the chair in the capacious boot, which also housed a cocktail cabinet and an icebox stuffed with champagne and caviar. Uncle Luigi had thought of everything and had no intention of stinting himself.

They set off. Along the coast road to Monte Carlo, through Beaulieu to Monaco and the palace of the principality on its high pinnacle, to the great bay and harbour of Monte Carlo, where a thousand yachts of a thousand millionaires dipped and swayed in the gentle eddies, and a hundred gramophones poured out Maurice Chevalier to the pampered darlings sprawled upon the decks:

> "Everee leetle breeze
> Seems to whispair Louise,
> Birds in the trees
> Seem to whispair Louise . . ."

Well, we're here, thought Rowbotham, as Charles brought the Duesenberg to a lubricious halt by the gilded portals of the Hôtel de Paris, where they were instantly attended by functionaries to the number of six, who brought out the crocodile-skin luggage, the wheelchair and Uncle Luigi.

Well, it's not gone too badly so far, continued Rowbotham to himself. The business on the Blue Train, that was a piece of bad luck and if it hadn't happened I should have no worries, no reservations whatsoever.

All in all, he continued to himself, this whole thing promises to go rather well, rather blandly. I mean, what other impediment? The search for the missing murderer on the train, that was a piece of pure bad luck, and will certainly never recur.

"We are in the Côte D'Azur, Uncle," he said, addressing the veiled figure, as the elevator swept them both, wheelchair and all, to their suite on the second floor, with the balcony that looked out on to the golden glory of the dying day. "And I'm sure everything's going to be as you wanted it from now on."

"Monsieur is perhaps not well?" hazarded the elevator man dubiously.

"Oh, he's fine," responded Rowbotham. "It's just that he's not very chatty, that's all."

The road that closely follows the river Rhone in some places hugs the foothills of les Barries beyond Orange; where the eighteen-thousand-odd feet of Mont de Lure rears up into the illimitable blueness to the eastward, where the cicadas twitter through day and night and the frogs croak in the rillets and runnels and the long damp grass from sunset to sunrise, there reposed by the gutter a large pantechnicon, what the English would call a station-wagon or a shooting-brake—anyhow, an admirably commodious vehicle to contain, as it did, four variously sized gentlemen and their baggage, which included two violin cases, a case for a cello and a similar repository for a double-bass. The vehicle was irremediably stuck by the roadside with a faint gush of steam being emitted from its working parts and one of the four gentlemen present—a slab-sided individual with a stomach that overhung his waist-belt by all of five inches—was peering anxiously into the open bonnet.

"We run outa water," he declared.

"I come to France," said one of his companions: a small man, but by his manner a large man inside. "I come to France, which, as I take it, is the heart of Western Art and Civilisation as we know it, with Cézanne, who happened just down the road, and this bum is telling me what is immediately discernible to anyone with an eye to see: namely that we have run out of water. And why have we run out of water, might one have the temerity to ask?"

"I—I kinda forgot to fill up at da last gas station, Nicky," said the offending creature.

"You forgot to fill up at the last gas station!" The blow

across the mouth that accompanied this declaration, aided, as it was, by a signet ring with a diamond the size of well-developed pea, and sharply faceted, scored a scarlet furrow. The big man, who could have hammered the little man into the ground a considerable distance with one downward blow of his massive fist, merely wiped away the blood and shed a tear.

"Nicky, what are we gonna do?" This from one of the others.

"This heap of garbage"—indicating the vehicle—"will not move for another half an hour, or possibly more," said the man Nicky, "on account of Elephant has driven it to the limit of its capacity, in and out, round about, for the last three hours and more, mostly without water. If it *ever* starts again, this has to be a miracle that is going to rival the Miracle of the Loaves and Fishes and all points west."

"So what do we do, Nicky?" The question came again.

"We wait till some bum comes along whose transport we can take a temporary lien upon," replied the other. "Meanwhile, we will open the bar. Make mine a bourbon and soda."

The suggestion was greeted with ovation by the man Nicky's companions. Even the one named Elephant, who was still bowed over the open bonnet and willing the red-hot engine to cool itself down and become again a viable appendage, perked up slightly when they took out the double-bass case and opened it to reveal—among other things—a veritable cocktail cabinet, with a miniature icebox and nibbles of roast peanuts, cheeses, biscuits, olives—both stuffed and unstuffed—and slivers of anchovies on toast. It should be added that, in addition to these comestibles and beverages, the capacious receptacle also contained a Thompson sub-machine-gun and six circular drums of .45-calibre ammunition of fifty rounds apiece.

"Here's to crime!" This was Nicky's invariable toast. The

others echoed his sentiment, downed their bourbon and filled up again.

Nicky's sharp, clever, ugly-handsome face relaxed, upon his second drink, from the expression of contempt and loathing that had been engendered by his minion Elephant and took upon itself an aspect reminiscent of that with which a young mother regards her first-born suckling at her erectile nipple.

"When I think of all that moolah," he declared, swilling the last of the bourbon and soda around the ice with a delicate twirl of his fingers. "When I think of that five million dollars . . ."

"Five and a half, Nicky," interposed one of his aides, not Elephant. "It has to be five and a half, Nicky. You're forgetting the Metropole Hotel heist which Luigi pulled off shortly before he handed in his chips. That has to be included."

"Abie, I stand corrected," replied Nicky, with more civility than was his wont. "The Metropole job must certainly have grossed out Luigi's stake by another half million bucks." He poured himself another three fingers of bourbon, ran his finger lovingly round one of the circular drums of .45-calibre ammunition. "And all of it ours—or *will* be ours."

Nicky's interlocutor in this dialogue, a tall and exceedingly thin man with a wall-eye, said: "There is the small matter of where the five and a half is stashed, Nicky. There is also the small matter of the Limey who is pushing him around. Who is pushing around what is left of Luigi, I mean."

"The Limey!" Nicky dismissed Ernest Rowbotham and all his works with a scrub-out of the hand. "The Limey presents no problem. The way our information is, the Limey must know where that loot left to him by his Uncle Luigi is hidden, and will think that it is safe. He will continue to think so"—here the finger (and an exceedingly delicate and well-manicured finger it was) once again stroked the ammunition drum—"until his premature passing and subsequent obsequies

—the which, out of delicacy, I think we shall have to attend.

"Dismiss the Limey, Abie. We shall tread him underfoot like a worm when the moment is opportune. All of you attend to me." His eyes—they were of the palest blue that is attributed to sensualists—flashed across his companions and held them to him. "*We* know very well that Luigi Gaudi never stashed that five and a half million in any bank. Luigi, why he never trusted any bank that much that he'd leave a dime on deposit. Why, he never entered a bank but half a dozen times in his whole life—and always then with a mask over his face and a pistol in his hand.

"The five and a half million (none of your half measures, Abie, fill her right up, and no soda this time) is undoubtedly on or about the person of Mr. Limey Rowbotham, or else this whole charade is to bring Mr. Limey Rowbotham into the proximity of the said fortune, which is stashed away in Monte Carlo without doubt, with full instructions to the nephew as to how and where to pick it up. Only, *we* shall pick it up. We shall pick it up—" he took a long pull at his drink and rolled the residuum round his mouth with a luxuriant languor, taking his time "—we shall pick it up, with the help of Mr. Limey Rowbotham."

"What if the guy doesn't come across, boss?" demanded one of the aides, an attenuated personage with a tall hat and a set of false teeth, which, since they could only have been family heirlooms, shifted with his slightest enunciation.

"If Mr. Limey Rowbotham does not come across, Boris," responded Nicky, "it will be because he does not know where the loot is stashed. No other answer will be acceptable. Your expertise in the matter of—er—persuasion leaves no doubt on that score. If he knows, he will squawk. If he does *not* know, your tender ministrations will convey him, in no very great haste, to his eternal rest."

The object of his comment, Boris, grinned and grossly displaced his false teeth. "Okay, boss," he said.

A flurry of rooks arising from the trees that skirted the bend in the road past which they had come heralded the present coming of a fair-sized motor car which, upon its approach, revealed itself to be carrying a man at the wheel and a lady passenger beside him.

"Here," said Nicky, "is the conveyance which—be the owners agreeable to the proposition, or be they not—will presently carry us the rest of the way to Monte Carlo."

And so it was.

CHAPTER 4

In the lobby of the Hôtel de Paris, Monte Carlo, there is a miniature equestrian statue of Louis XIV in much the same pose as that in which that egregious monarch presents himself in the forecourt of his masterpiece, which is the Palace of Versailles. Placed there in 1907, the statue quickly gained for itself a reputation as a good-luck charm amongst the inveterate, regular gamblers at the Casino, and the raised knee of Le Roi Soleil's charger has been rubbed for good luck so that it shines to this day like a good deed in a naughty world. They were passing through the lobby, the "regulars," and taking a rub of Louis XIV's mount's knee, when Ernest Rowbotham, followed by chauffeur Charles pushing Uncle Luigi, followed by porters to the number of six carrying the baggage, proceeded to the ancient and elegant elevator which conveyed them to a balconied suite on the second floor which had lately been the love-nest of King Edward VII, his various *amies* and other crowned heads.

Alone again with the stiff and unresponsive figure in the wheelchair, Ernest poured them both a glass of champagne, plastered ikra caviar on a pile of blinis and opened the second of the envelopes which the lawyers Messrs. Platts, Brinkley, Hobbs, Hobbs and Bailey had provided him with. This bore the legend: *Read upon arrival at Monte Carlo.*

The instructions therein were brief and unequivocal:

Dress: White tie and tails.
Venue: The Salles Privées at the Casino.
Object: You will stake the maximum 10,000 francs on any of the *chances simples* of your choice, and continue to do so till you have either broken the bank or lost a total of 100,000 francs. Simultaneously, in the same play, you will stake the maximum of 600 francs *en plein* on number 13, and continue to do so till you have either broken the bank or lost a total of 6,000 francs. The Casino has been instructed. Funds await you there.

Nibbling at his caviar, sipping at his Krug '24, Rowbotham read and re-read the missive, which, carrying with it as it did a faint whiff of legalese and with none of the homely overtones of Uncle Luigi's valedictory letter, suggested that it had been cobbled together in the offices of Messrs. Platts, Brinkley, Hobbs, Hobbs and Bailey to Uncle's broad instruction.

But what, he asked himself, was a *chance simple?* And what *en plein?* And how was it that the maximum stakes allowable were at such a variance? He wished now that he had had the foresight (and *surely* he should have guessed that a visit to Monte Carlo must mean the gambling tables) to provide himself with some information on the system of roulette. He would feel such a fool at the table, having to ask someone how to place the bets, with experienced gamblers sneering from behind their long cigarette holders no doubt, beautiful women turning their heads away in contempt and Uncle Luigi blindly gazing at him . . .

He poured himself another glass of champagne.

The hell with it, he presently told himself, for he was a man who could reason things out, and expensive wine was no bar to the process. One presumed that the figures mentioned in the instructions, that's to say a total of one hundred and six thousand francs which he was permitted to lose, was something that did not occur on every wet Thursday afternoon—not even in Monte Carlo. It was a sum that, surely, carried some weight. Well might he appear to be a novice, but if a novice, then a novice with a very resounding wallet, which (this he posed to himself with the slight stirrings of carnal lust) should greatly commend him to the beautiful women. His ignorance would surely pass almost unnoticed as he scattered francs upon the table to the amazement and admiration of the *bon ton*.

He recalled the famous music hall song, and sang the chorus in his shaky baritone:

"*As I walk along the Bois de Boulogne with an independent air,*
You can hear the girls declare: 'He must be a millionaire,'
Oh, and then they sigh and wish to die. And they turn and wink the other eye . . .
THE MAN WHO BROKE THE BANK AT MONTE CA-A-A-R-R-LO!"

He drained Uncle Luigi's glass and poured them both another.

The Monte Carlo Casino, whose twin towers provide a mark for passing ships as useful as any lighthouses in the world, was almost totally rebuilt in the late 1870s by Charles Garnier, the architect of that delicious wedding cake topped off with apple crumble and cream known as the Paris Opera House. When Charles the chauffeur brought them to the ornate flight of steps leading up into the sugar-plum edifice, a group of functionaries of the establishment came forward to greet their arrival. They comprised the Director-General, the Sub-Director, two ordinary directors and three faceless creatures of the sort which that sort of folk seem to need to have about them all the time.

"Ah, messieurs, such an honour!" The Director-General was hung about with bits and pieces of various grades of the Légion d'honneur and had appallingly bad breath. He glanced dubiously at Uncle Luigi, who—clad with some difficulty by Rowbotham in a Savile Row tailcoat suit with a starched shirt-front and white tie, but still wearing the broad-brimmed slouch hat, with head bowed and hands folded on his lap—predictably made no response to the effusion. Well might the four massive bronze and gold caryatids who supported the vaulted roof of the auditorium, and the two naked youths sculptured below them who gazed down with epicene intensity, have felt rebuffed: Uncle Luigi, carefully borne in his wheelchair by the dutiful Charles, paid neither them nor the distinguished welcoming committee the slightest attention.

"*Alors, messieurs, les salles privées!*" The Director-General did it with a great amount of style. He had obviously been disappointed, not to say affronted, by Uncle Luigi's lack of response, and it could not have escaped his notice that Ernest Rowbotham's imbibing of Krug '24 had in no way improved his gait, not to say his articulation.

They were ushered to one of the tables where play was in progress. Uncle Luigi's chair was wheeled to a place of honour at the edge of the game, and Rowbotham given a seat beside him. A flunky in tailcoat with brass buttons laid at his elbow a silver tray bearing three piles of coloured chips. "Monsieur's stake for the night," he murmured. This was the hundred and six thousand francs.

The Director-General and his aides retired, bowing, and left them to it. Rowbotham, his mind curiously clear behind the mist of alcohol that seemed to obtrude between himself and the rest of the world was happily conscious that their arrival seemed hardly to have caused the slightest interest among the players gathered about their table. A few eyebrows had been raised at the sight of the masked figure in the hat; but Monte Carlo is nothing if not the last resting place of eccentrics, and with the next spin of the wheel, Rowbotham and Uncle Luigi were just part of the furniture.

"*Messieurs, faites vos jeux.*" The Monte Carlo Casino does not acknowledge the presence of ladies, though they are always there in abundance. While making this invitation, the croupier in charge of the wheel set the thing in motion with a brisk turn of the cruciform handle, at the same time throwing the white ball into the revolving basin.

Rowbotham picked up a handful of chips and counted out two piles of ten thousand and six hundred respectively. After that he was stuck for ideas.

"Can I be of aid, sir?" The speaker was at his elbow, and his voice had overtones of a pleasant transatlantic burr. He was perhaps about fifty: well-tended moustache, an expensive-looking sun-tan, dandified as to dress with an embroidered velvet waistcoat in white silk under his tailcoat. Rowbotham took to him at once.

"I—I want to put the maximum on thirteen," he faltered. "Likewise the maximum on a *chance simple*—whatever that is."

"Nothing easier, sir." Taking the smaller of the two piles that Rowbotham had counted out, his new friend placed them in the square on the green baize cloth that was lettered with the number thirteen. "As to *chances simples*, you have the choice of odds and evens, red or black, low or high. It's an even-money bet any way. Take your pick."

Rowbotham put the ten thousand in the space marked with a red diamond, which was right by his elbow.

"Here goes, Uncle Luigi," he murmured.

The little white ball, robbed of momentum by the slowing of the wheel, began its descent. Moments later, it struck the first of the diamond-shaped studs that encircled the basin and its movements became erratic, fickle.

"*Les jeux sont faits. Rien ne va plus,*" intoned the croupier. The last of the bets, laid there by those who fondly imagined that the Goddess of Chance smiles upon late-comers, had been placed. Click-click, click-click—and the ball finally reposed itself in one of the numbered compartments.

"*Quinze, rouge, impair et manque.*"

"You've won," said Rowbotham's new friend. "Beginner's luck, I guess."

"Couldn't be more so," confessed Rowbotham, staring in fascination as a croupier counted out a pile of chips and shovelled them over to him with devastating expertise admixed with a certain casual contempt. "Believe it or not, this is the first time I've ever played roulette."

"You don't say," commented the other. "Now, this interests me. Here are you, if I may say so without giving offence, with not the slightest idea, not knowing one end of the table from the other, nor how to lay a bet—and you go straight into maximum stakes. You realise, do you, that if your *en plein* on thirteen had come up, you'd have netted twenty-one thousand at thirty-five times the amount of your stake?"

"No, I didn't—but I'm grateful for the information. By the way, my name's Ernest Rowbotham."

"I'm Ezekiel Bragg. My friends call me Zeke."

They shook hands. There was an awkward moment as both of them glanced at the still figure in the wheelchair.

"My uncle," said Rowbotham lamely. "He's—um—a bit deaf and not very communicative. He just watches things. You'll have to forgive him."

"Pleased to meet you, sir," said Bragg loudly, and predictably received no response.

"*Messieurs, faites vos jeux.*"

"I'm going on thirteen again," said Rowbotham, "but I shall go on black this time instead of red, so that I shall pick up the whole boodle if black thirteen comes up."

"You're learning fast, Ernest," said his new friend. "Yes, sir. You're learning fast."

"*Les jeux sont faits. Rien ne va plus.*"

Rowbotham relaxed. It seemed to him that he had been at this game all his life. He was, he appreciated in a sparkling flash of insight, a natural-born gambler. And dead lucky. Why, for heaven's sake, had he laboured for so long in the vineyards of lower private education for a pittance when he might have come to this fruition and doubled his stake every night of his life?

Across the table, he met the eye of a young woman whose distinctly unprepossessing appearance was familiar: hair in "buns," steel-rimmed glasses, and she was wearing a kind of gunny-sack tied round the middle with string. She was also watching him closely, and, as their gaze was joined, she lowered her eyes and made an entry in the notebook at her elbow. For some reason that he could not fathom, her presence—the presence of, he remembered her now, Miss Annabel Smith, "agent"—came as an unaccountable depressant.

The white ball clattered neatly to a halt.

"*Dix-neuf, rouge, impair et passe.*"

He watched in dismay as the piles of chips—*his* chips—were scooped away with the same contemptuous authority with which they had lately been delivered.

"Can't win all the time, Ernest," commented his new friend.

In the event, Rowbotham's first evening at the gaming tables was a total fiasco. His ingenuous belief that an even bet was a push-over, or was at least an enterprise that could, at worst, only leave one broken even, was speedily disabused when a run of five reds in a row and a couple of zeros to the bank cleared him of his ten thousand francs dedicated to *chances simples*. Number thirteen simply never came up all evening. When the last of his chips was gone, he turned to Mr. Ezekiel ("Zeke") Bragg, who had amassed a small pile by playing a more *soigné* staking system *à cheval, transversale* and *carré*, the ins and outs of which he explained to his disciple.

"You must think I'm a most awful mug," said Rowbotham.

"Your staking is a little on the rigid side," admitted the other. "But, I have to tell you that, at bottom, there's really no way, no way at all, save for sheer good chance, to win at the tables. The advantages are stacked in favour of the house. Right down the line. Despite that"—he indicated the folks sitting round the table—"there's scarcely one here who doesn't believe, deep down, that there's an infallible system just waiting to be discovered."

"You'd think that the penny would drop eventually," said Rowbotham. "I mean, if they play here regularly and see that the house always wins in the end."

Ezekiel Bragg shook his head. "Human nature," he said, "in the face of continued, best evidence, will not accept such a proposition. Who, my dear Ernest, would you suppose, among all the people here present, are best equipped, by experience, to discern that, despite the siren calls of chance, this is a mug's game, pure and simple.

"Why—um—the croupiers, I suppose," essayed Rowbotham. "They see folks like me going broke every night, and must be laughing up their sleeves."

"They also see occasional, fantastic runs of luck," replied his interlocutor. "There are and have been a few, a very few, who have made consistent fortunes on the tables. Such people do not pass unnoticed by the croupiers, and their good luck wipes clean from the minds of these gentlemen the stern logic that with the rare—and mathematically calculable—exceptions, the house will frequently win in the short term and *always* in the long term. Do you know what the Monte Carlo croupiers do on their days off, their free days?"

"No. Tell me."

"They are not allowed to play at table in their own casino, so what do they do? They trot down the road to the Cannes Casino and play out the same kind of fantasies about the ever-elusive 'infallible system' which they see mugs like you and me failing at every day of their working lives at the tables."

"Very depressing," said Rowbotham.

"All is not lost," replied Ezekiel Bragg lightly, scooping up a comfortable pile of fairly high-denomination chips. "This evening has been quite exceptional for me. I think you and your uncle have brought me luck. It may last. It may not. In any event, let us take fortune on the flood. I am buying the champagne. To the bar, my dear Ernest, to the bar!"

They proceeded to the bar, Ezekiel Bragg leading, his arm tucked into that of Ernest Rowbotham and engaging him in anecdotes both well authenticated and apocryphal about the Monte Carlo Casino, while Uncle Luigi followed after, propelled by the chauffeur Charles.

What Rowbotham did not immediately notice, not till they had all taken their seats at table in the bar, was that the ubiquitous Miss Annabel Smith had followed them in and was sitting at a far corner of the room, notebook at her elbow, myopic eyes fixed upon them.

There was also a quartette of rather boozed gentlemen of clearly transatlantic provenance sitting at the next table, whose rumbustious conversation flagged and died when Ezekiel Bragg, having ordered champagne, proceeded to give

Rowbotham and Uncle Luigi a dissertation upon the Principality of Monaco, the founding of the Casino, its difficult, not to say disastrous, beginnings, to its present fame and fortune. These four Americans—one was built like a house, another tall and thin and wall-eyed, another short and stout, and the last a small man of almost Napoleonic presence—listened quite unashamedly to the peroration. But, then, Ezekiel Bragg was one hell of a good talker.

They parted company at two o'clock in the morning. Charles settled Uncle Luigi in the rear of the Duesenberg, Rowbotham and Bragg shook hands and promised—with the half sincerity of the half drunk and euphoric—to keep in touch with each other. It was "Good night, Ern. Great night." And "Good night, Zeke. Thanks for all your help and advice."

Rowbotham unsteadily joined his uncle in their limousine. It was by chance that, as the Duesenberg circled the ornamental garden facing the Casino, Rowbotham turned to see Miss Annabel Smith enter a taxi and follow after them.

"Not straight back to the hotel, Charles," he said. "Take us along the Nice road, where my uncle can admire the views."

"*Oui, m'sieu.*"

It was a right turn to the hotel, a left turn towards Nice. Looking back, it seemed to Rowbotham that the following taxi, after half committing itself to the right, followed them to the left as if at a last-minute instruction.

"The bitch, whoever she is, is spying on us!"

"*Pardon, m'sieu?*"

"Nothing, Charles. *Continuez.*"

"*Oui, m'sieu.*"

The cicadas trilled out there in the sage, and the edge of the long Mediterranean whispered at the foot of the craggy cliffs below; a full moon glowed against the absurd backdrop of deep azure and uncountable stars of every magnitude; the scents of honeysuckle, wisteria, frangipani, and the myriads of tiny plants that clung to the dry, sloping, stony soil of the coastline were fit to make the mind abandon itself to pleasure unannealed. Rowbotham resisted the siren call; addressed himself to the matter uppermost in his thoughts.

"Pull in here, Charles," he said at length. "My uncle will wish to admire the lights of Monte Carlo from this excellent viewpoint."

The chauffeur obeyed. The Duesenberg rolled grandly to a halt in a lay-by. Before Charles had snicked on the hand brake, the Monte Carlo taxi swept past them along the straight stretch of the Corniche that Rowbotham had chosen for his experiment. Half a mile or so further on, maybe less, it pulled into the side of the road and, hiding itself into a similar lay-by, switched off lights.

"It's very pretty here, Uncle, don't you think?" asked Rowbotham.

The ghost of Uncle Luigi Gaudi could not, surely, have been insensitive to the sweep of the bay behind them, to the necklace of lights beginning at the Spélugues Promontory, which bears the palace of the Principality and seat of Monaco, Monte Carlo beyond and all the yachts in the harbour, the eternal stars above.

"I think my uncle is possibly rather cold, Charles," declared Rowbotham. "Take us to the Paris. At rather a smart pace. *Très vite.*"

"*Oui, m'sieu.*"

Rowbotham looked back as Charles did a U-turn and, pulling out of the lay-by, headed back to Monte Carlo with all the power of the Duesenberg's eight cylinders at full stretch. He saw the taxi's lights flare on, saw it take a U-turn and come back after them.

"Keep it like this, Charles," he said. "*Mon oncle, il adore la vitesse.*"

"*Oui, m'sieu.*"

The Royal Suite at the Paris possessed—in addition to two bedrooms, a sitting-room and drawing-room, a balcony overlooking the lush garden, and a marvellously fitted-out kitchen —a bathroom of truly oriental opulence, done out in the Turkish style, or possibly Algerian, with blue and white tiles, a sunken bath, a huge handbasin in the centre of which a naked alabaster nymph bore on high a conch shell from which poured a constant fountain of pure water.

It was in the bathroom that Rowbotham had decided to accommodate Uncle Luigi. There being no specific instructions on the point, he could not bring himself to undress the corpse again, put it into its silk pyjamas, lift it into bed. Accordingly, he wheeled his charge into the bathroom and left him there, facing the wall, still, silent, perfectly at rest.

"Good night, Uncle," he said. "Hope you enjoyed your night out. See you tomorrow. But, first, I've got to sort out little Miss Annabel Smith and discover what *she's* up to."

He connected with the hall porter.

"*Allô?*"

"Listen, this is Rowbotham, Royal Suite. I take it you speak English."

"Of course, m'sieu."

"Well, I chanced to see a young lady in the lobby this evening. I'm almost sure that we have met before, but it would be an embarrassment to me and no doubt an annoyance to her if I approached her and mistakenly claimed an acquaintance. Do you follow me?"

"Of course, m'sieu." (The French understand these things perfectly.)

"Her name—that's to say the name of the lady with whom I have a past acquaintance—is Miss Annabel Smith. Could it possibly be she, staying here in the hotel?"

A few moments' pause.

"Yes, m'sieu, Miss Annabel Smith. Room three-seventeen. Shall I connect you?"

"Oh, no, no. I will approach her tomorrow, possibly at luncheon. Thank you so much. Good night."

"Good night, m'sieu."

Rowbotham replaced the receiver and addressed his reflection in the Florentine mirror opposite. Did his jawline not seem less weak than it had in the days of his schoolmastering? He thought it did. Opulence—the Blue Train, the Hôtel de Paris, losing a hundred and six thousand francs in an evening without turning a hair—all this certainly brought out the best in a chap. He hitched his bow-tie, flapped his tails and went off to deal with little Miss Annabel Smith.

Room 317 was on the floor above. In answer to his knock, there presently came a reply: "Who is it?"

"My name's Rowbotham. I think you know me. I should like a few words with you."

After a discernible pause, the door was opened by a woman in a peignoir. Her hair cascaded over her shoulders in a well-groomed cloud. The edges of the peignoir were held together with fingers of slender elegance and quite unbelievable length, but not so closely as to hide from his gaze the inner slopes of tremendous promise. Rowbotham, who felt his manhood stir, transferred his regard from the woman's bosom to her eyes, which were of a misty, fugitive blueness, totally enticing.

"I'm most awfully sorry," he faltered. "I came to see Miss Smith. I had—um—a few questions to put to her."

"Come in," she replied.

He followed her into a suite that was scarcely less opulent than that in which King Edward VII had disported. She pointed to a tray of drinks on a Louis Seize console table.

"Build yourself something," she said. "I'll be back. Mine's a Scotch and water."

She went.

In the process of building her a Scotch and water and himself a glass of Indian tonic water (he was by now hideously conscious that the world was all akilter and it was probably on account of all the alcohol he had ingested that evening), Rowbotham muzzily tried to come to terms with a concept that seemed to link the frumpish Miss Annabel Smith with the luscious creature—she of the tumbled hair, the opulent breasts, the promising eyes—whom he had just met.

His unsteady hands making a slightly protracted job of fixing the drinks, his no less unsteady mind juggling with his new concept, the job was scarcely finished before his hostess returned.

Her luxuriant hair was now bundled into a kind of mobcap. The wildly appetizing figure was buried beneath a terrytowel bath robe. The eyes were hidden behind steel-rimmed glasses. She carried a thick cardboard file under her right arm. There was a sharpened pencil over her left ear.

"Miss Smith!" exclaimed Rowbotham, adding lamely, "er—here's your Scotch and water. Hope there's not too much water."

"It looks about the right colour," she said, taking the glass. "Well, your very good health."

"And yours," murmured Rowbotham.

They both drank, and she watched him over the rim of her glass.

He felt that the ball was in his court; he played it:

"You have been following me—us—around ever since the Blue Train," he said. "Don't deny it. You were watching us at the Casino, you followed us along the Corniche and back. And you are booked into our hotel. I saw you come in tonight and check that I had taken my keys from the pigeon-hole. Deny it if you can."

"True," she replied blandly.

"Why? *Why* are you following me—us?"

"Sit down, Mr. Rowbotham," she said, doing likewise and crossing her legs so that, for a brief instant, the whole length of them was visible from under the opening of the terry-cloth robe.

"Why?" he repeated, with much less authority than previously.

"Mr. Rowbotham—" at this juncture, she opened the file, adjusted her glasses to the end of her nose and gazed at him with some severity. "I am, in addition to being an attorney-at-law, a director of the Universal Dogs' Home of Cincinnati."

"Aaaah!"

"You have heard of us." It was not a question.

"You're the folks who—"

"We are the folks who, if you do not carry out the provisions of your late uncle Mr. Luigi Gaudi's will, succeed to the entire fortune by default."

"Dogs, I don't like," said Rowbotham. "They are flea-infested fur bags full of horrid diseases and they make a hell of a mess in streets and parks. In Paris particularly, from my experience, and Bath is scarcely better. Still, I suppose it must have been a considerable blow to you when I accepted Uncle Luigi's terms and you lost the fortune."

The eyes, over the steel-rimmed spectacles, were unwavering.

"We have not *yet* lost the fortune, Mr. Rowbotham," she said.

Rowbotham laughed shortly. "Oh, come now, Miss Smith," he said, gently chiding. "A joke is a joke. You must know very well that, by my agreeing to my uncle's last wish, I have totally excluded the—what do you call yourselves? . . ."

"The Universal Dogs' Home of Cincinnati," responded Miss Annabel Smith. "And we are not totally excluded. We are not by a very long way excluded at all—as I will explain to you."

Rowbotham had the very clear sensation that either someone had walked over his grave, or that he was back at—or imminently due to go back to—Hillbrough Hall College for the Sons of Christian Gentlemen.

"Do you—do you mind if I pour myself another drink, Miss Smith?" he asked, rising.

"Do so, Mr. Rowbotham," she replied. "And I would advise a fairly stiff one, because you are going to need it. And while you're about it, will you please freshen my glass?"

She began by reading him a piece from Shakespeare's *The Merchant of Venice*, which he knew quite well, having studied it for his School Certificate. She read impressively from a calf-bound volume of The Complete Works with a lot of heavy gilt tooling on the spine.

> "Therefore prepare thee to cut off the flesh.
> Shed thou no blood, nor cut thou less nor more
> But just a pound of flesh. If thou tak'st more
> Or less than just a pound—be it but so much
> As makes it light or heavy in the substance
> Or the division of the twentieth part
> Of one poor scruple; nay, if the scale do turn
> But in the estimation of a hair—
> Thou diest, and all thy goods are confiscate."

"You should have been an actress," said Rowbotham, for want of something better to say. "And just what is the point you are attempting to convey?"

She took a sip of her drink and said: "Portia's courtroom speech, which totally confounded Shylock, is very apposite to our present situation. The lawyers Platts, Brinkley, Hobbs, Hobbs and Bailey, who drew up the terms of Luigi Gaudi's will, must have given the job to the office-boy. Through that will, Mr. Rowbotham, one could quite easily drive a coach and horses—as I was happy to report to my fellow directors of the Universal Dogs' Home of Cincinnati."

"Oh," said Rowbotham, and now he quite clearly saw himself back in some dreadful private school, faced by serried rows of brutish dullards all smelling of chewing gum and feet. "Please continue."

"The terms of the will are too precise, and at the same time too imprecise—like the terms of Shylock's bond, which set out a pound of the Merchant's flesh on the non-payment of the loan, but made no allowance for the shedding of blood, nor for any slight error of weight in the cutting of the flesh. Do you follow me, Mr. Rowbotham?"

Rowbotham nodded. "I begin to get your drift, Miss Smith."

She tapped the file on her knee. "We have a copy of the will, together with copies of the instructions that have been given to you concerning the itinerary that Luigi Gaudi drew up for his—how to put it?—posthumous entertainment. Two points emerge."

"And what are they?" asked Rowbotham, his last hopes ebbing, like sand through the eyeholes of his patent leather shoes, before the steady gaze of that formidable woman.

"First, you have seven envelopes for the seven days of the week," said Miss Smith. "You will open them day by day and perform the services therein specified—as tonight you took the corpse of Luigi Gaudi, dressed in tails as specified, to the Casino, there to play a stake of one hundred and six thousand francs in a specified manner. Correct?"

Rowbotham nodded miserably. This voluptuous young woman, overlaid as she was by a shapeless bath robe, magnificent mane of hair scrunched up under a mob-cap, uncomely specs perched on the end of her Grecian nose, was a human juggernaut who was ploughing his dreams into the dust.

"Tomorrow, you will open the second envelope," said Miss Smith, and will carry out the instructions therein with no doubt the same devotion as before. I shall be there to watch you do it."

Rowbotham, who had opted for a very stiff whisky upon her advice, still retained a residuum of spirit—though it could be said to be of the distilled sort. He pointed to her, squinting along his extended forefinger.

"And if I step out of line in any respect," he said, "you will dish me out of the fortune and have it reverted to the Universal Dogs' Home of Cincinnati. Do I have it right?"

She smiled—rather thinly. "Precisely," she retorted. "You see, it is the Portia principle: because the terms of the will were drawn up by an office-boy, you have no room for manoeuvre. Let your Uncle Luigi be wearing a black tie when he had specified a white, let you but place your bet *en plein* on fourteen instead of thirteen, let you deviate in any detail from the letter of the will, and I shall apply to the court for a reversion of the fortune to the U.D.H.O.C.—*and get it, Mr. Rowbotham!*"

Rowbotham's spirit had, oddly enough, been strengthened during her late peroration. He saw—he thought he saw—the weakness of her argument and her stance.

"You won't catch me out," he said. "I'm a very precise person. When I was a little boy, my mother always served apple batter pudding on Mondays, Mondays was apple-batter pudding day. Once, when Mother served treacle tart for pudding on a Monday, I sulked for the rest of the week: she never did it again. Likewise, when I go to bed at night, I place the contents of my pockets and my person in this order on the dressing table: watch to the left, cuff-links to the right, comb at the top, loose change in the middle, rolled-up tie below, wallet on top of the loose change. To deviate from this procedure in any respect would cause me a sleepless night. So you see, Miss Smith, I am almost uniquely fitted to carry out my late uncle's last request. You may follow me around and take notes as you will—if I can't carry out specific instructions for the next six days, nobody can!" He sat back in his chair, drained his drink and treated Annabel Smith to a smug leer.

She appeared in no way disconcerted. "As I have already indicated," she said, "two points are involved in this issue. The first is the precision with which, in order to fulfil the terms of this appallingly badly drawn-up will, you are obliged to conform—"

"And shall, and shall," he interposed, chuckling. "And at the end of the week, I shall be free of you, dear Miss Smith."

"Not so," she replied.

"Huh?"

"It doesn't end with the end of the week, Mr. Rowbotham," she said quietly.

"Oh, yes it does!"

She shook her head.

Once again, Rowbotham saw a pit yawning at his feet, with loutish smelly schoolboys, grey beef stew that looked like boiled elephant, a miserable pittance of a salary.

"It—it doesn't?" he whispered.

"No. Thanks to the tender ministrations of Platts, Brinkley, Hobbs, Hobbs and Bailey, the conditions upon which you accepted your late uncle as a companion have no point of termination. In short, Mr. Rowbotham, you are stuck with that corpse for life."

"For *life?*"

"Absolutely."

"But—"

"There are no buts, Mr. Rowbotham. By the terms of the will, as drawn up by Platts, Brinkley, Hobbs, Hobbs and Bailey, you have no release from the agreement upon which you have entered, save to revert the fortune to the U.D.H.O.C. As I shall successfully plead in court, the seven days in question have no end. If you stay by your pledge, you must repeat the instructions contained in the seven envelopes to perpetuity, that's to say to the end of your life, if you wish to retain the fortune. Week after week, Mr. Rowbotham, you will have to tout your uncle's mummified corpse through the seven days of hedonism that he determined for himself. There is no let-out for you. From Monday through Sunday, you will have to peddle that corpse through the high life of Monte Carlo, to the Casino, the ballets, this and that and wherever. And I, Mr. Rowbotham, will be watching you for the slightest diversion from what I have called the Portia principle. And when I have retired from the board of the U.D.H.O.C., someone else will take on the task of monitoring you till the end of your life.

"Would you like another drink?"

"I think I could do with one," said Ernest Rowbotham weakly.

CHAPTER 5

Commissaire Paul Darré's wife was devoutly religious, ardently in love with him and in possession of a total inability to remember dates. That morning, she had rung him at the Préfecture to confirm that she was indeed *enceinte* of their ninth child. When his assistant Martin came in at about eleven o'clock, Darré was having a by no means habitual tot of cognac to steady his nerves after making a rough calculation of his salary *vis-à-vis* his bank balance, house mortgage and other credit commitments, the price of kids' footwear, and so forth.

"Anything the matter, Chief?" asked Martin. Martin, unlike his superior, was tall and gangling, the other was short and stocky—indeed, running to plump. It was not known to either of them that they were generally known in the department, behind their backs, as Laurel and Hardy.

"Should there be?" growled Darré.

"Sorry. I only asked," replied the other.

"Well, what is it?"

"It's the car we found abandoned nearby the Casino last evening, Chief. We traced it to a Monsieur Claude Haquin, owner, who lives in Montélimar."

"And? There must be more, Martin. You are looking at me with the intensity of a conjuror who is just about to produce a rabbit out of a hat."

Martin took upon himself the slightly deflated look of one who has been pipped in the act of delivering a surprise.

Sulkily, he said: "I just had a call from Orange. They found an abandoned car by the wayside just out of town. It had run out of gas. Nearby, in the heather, they found a man and woman. Dead. Shot. And the man has been identified as Charles Haquin, owner of the other car—*our* car."

"The woman—his wife?"

"No. One Thérèse Fouquet. A whore. Also resident of Montélimar."

"Anything on the abandoned car?"

"That was stolen in Clermont-Ferrand the day before yesterday, from outside a bank. Witnesses have been found who saw four men get into it and drive off, the owner having obligingly left it unlocked with the keys in the ignition."

Darré poured himself another tot and one for Martin; shoved the other glass across his desk towards his assistant.

"How do you read it?" he asked.

"Thanks, Chief," said the other. "Well, I see it this way: the Haquin character is off down to the coast for a dirty weekend with his regular tart from the local brothel. On the road out of Orange, they come upon four types with a stolen car that's run out of gas. Maybe they pull in to offer help. Maybe they're flagged down. In any event, their car is commandeered—and they are shot."

"These four types must be of a very desperate nature," vouchsafed Darré.

"You don't know the half of it, Chief," responded his assistant. "The Orange fellows found no less than sixteen spent forty-five-calibre cartridge cases on the scene of the murders. Haquin and his tart were pretty nearly cut in half, both. It had to be a sub-machine-gun. A Thompson, most likely."

"A tommy-gun!" cried Darré. "Has Chicago come to the Midi, then?"

The question was merely rhetorical, but, though unintentionally, could hardly have been more prescient.

"Oh, Uncle Luigi—this is going too far! *This* is a bit much!"

Rowbotham had opened the envelope containing his instructions for the day, it being noon, and he had scarcely woken and the rummage of the drink he had imbibed the night before was rattling around in his cranium like pebbles in a coconut shell.

Uncle Luigi made no response, but continued to stare blindly through his mask and under his hat.

Rowbotham re-read his instructions.

Dress: Dove grey suits. Fancy vests. Spats. Dark red carnation buttonholes.
Venue: The best Thé Dansant in town, where the high-priced whores hang out.
Object: Have a few dances. Pick out the best-looking whore in the joint. (She has to be a redhead.) Back to her place. And I want to watch.

"You are a *filthy* old corpse, Uncle!" declared Rowbotham. He weaved an unsteady course to the telephone and ordered black coffee.

The two dove grey suits had been fashioned, like the rest of their ensembles, by a long-established tailor's in Savile Row, London, who had clad crowned heads of the world since before the French Revolution. The fancy vests (or waistcoats as Rowbotham and his fellow Britons called them) had presented slightly more of a problem, for Savile Row would not touch such sartorial confectionery with a barge pole. However, upon receiving his uncle's shopping list, Rowbotham had found a little tailor in Whitechapel who specialised in fancy vests and like accessories that are generally associated with co-respondents, actors, commercial travellers and others of a similarly raffish nature.

The dark red carnations presented no problem: Rowbotham purchased them from the excellent florist's shop in the palatial lobby of the hotel. Miss Annabel Smith was there, sitting in an armchair and reading a book. She addressed him:

"The best *thé dansant* in town is at the Café Grimaldi," she said. "It begins at three. I have duplicates of all your sealed envelopes."

"You will be present, of course," said Rowbotham.

"Naturally. As to the matter of the redhead, I will concede that she need not necessarily be a natural. Henna will do. But red she must be. Have a good time."

"I will do my best," said Rowbotham.

He ordered the Duesenberg for three, and Charles duly deposited Uncle Luigi in the back of the limousine. They set off for the Café Grimaldi, and Miss Annabel Smith followed after in a taxi.

The Café Grimaldi lay within a stone's throw of the Casino, and had a charming patio overlooking the plage, where swallow-tailed waiters served *thé à l'anglaise* under the striped awnings: delicate cucumber sandwiches, paper thin after the English manner, mouth-watering cakes both seed and plum, together with more robust fare for the adventurous, such as salmon and salad, prunes and custard, egg and anchovy, Eccles cakes, the elegant chocolate-covered éclairs. And, of course, tea—Chinese and Indian. These delightful comestibles could also be consumed in the shadowed coolness of the *salle de danse,* at discreet tables set in niches round the walls, where one could view the dancers circling the miniscule floor to the music of the tango, the foxtrot and the quickstep, played by a quartette of violin, clarinet, piano-accordion and drums, who called themselves Mr. Freddie et ses Boys; Freddie it was who played violin and occasionally made some shift to dictate the tempi. The tea dance, essentially a product of the English mating ritual, had exported well to France, where it was destined to survive long after the native fruit had whithered on the vine.

Rowbotham opted to go inside, so Charles the chauffeur wheeled Uncle Luigi to a corner table, bowed to both and left them.

Rowbotham looked about him.

"Well, there are plenty of seemingly unattached ladies here, Uncle," he said. "How many of them are on the game it would be difficult to determine, since they all look basically alike: over-dressed and highly painted. Do I espy a redhead? By jove, yes, I do! Oh, my God—how do I go about this?"

(It has to be stated that Ernest Rowbotham's experience with women outside of the unfortunate incident with the virginal Felicity Thorseby—could be expressed in one word. And that word was "nil.")

It was at this moment of indecision that he saw Miss Annabel Smith enter the room to be shown to a table opposite from where he and Uncle Luigi were placed, with a clear view of Rowbotham's comings and goings. She was dressed in a variant of the gunny-sack and her hair was back in the earphones. He tried to assemble—for some wayward reason that he could not have fathomed even had he tried—the vision of the creature who had opened her door to him the previous night: she of the hair, the eyes, the Foothills of Promise—but it would not come. Miss Smith settled herself down, ordered her tea, took her notebook from out of her handbag and awaited events.

"What I am going to do, Uncle," said Rowbotham, "is to approach the red-haired lady yonder and ask her for a dance. Oddly enough, I have never danced with a lady, though I pride myself on being a bit of an expert at the tango. Ernest the demon tango-ist of the Palais de Danse! It happened this way: when I was games master at that school near Newmarket, I was also expected to teach the louts to dance. This I did by obtaining a handbook entitled *Modern Dancing in 12 Easy Lessons*, by Gertrude Heffer. Armed with this admirable work of reference, I quickly made myself adept at the art, and indeed discovered that I had a decided talent for it. In all, I suppose I must have taught upwards of sixty boys to *chassé*, dip and bend, trail a foot, reverse turn. All those ghastly, smelly, sniggering little beasts. And I never yet danced with a woman.

"I think, after all, Uncle, that your idea for this evening wasn't such a bad idea after all."

He got up, buttoned the jacket of his dove grey suit and strode purposefully across the floor to where sat the redhead. Miss Annabel Smith picked up her pencil and made a brief entry in her notebook.

"*Excusez-moi, mademoiselle. Voulez-vous desire de danser avec moi?*" Rowbotham had that kind of English-schoolboy French at his nimble fingertips.

"Be a pleasure, ducks." The redhead was tiny, but voluptuous as to build nevertheless, dressed in a sequinned sheath-dress about two sizes too small, and spoke with the authentic cockney accent of those who have been born within the sound of Bow-bells.

"Well, how nice," said Rowbotham, "to meet a fellow countryman—woman."

Mr. Freddie et ses Boys struck up the famous tango "La Composita," and Rowbotham was immediately in his element. To the scratchy tune of this deathless number, played on the school gramophone (with Jones Minor, who on account of his obesity and tendency to incontinence was excused games and dancing, delegated to rewind when the thing ran down), had he not taught a whole generation of shuffling hobbledehoys to rival in pantherine suavity any South American gigolo?

The redhead was immediately impressed. "Oooh—you can tango, you reely can!" she declared.

"I learned it," said Rowbotham, "in Rio de Janeiro. It's the only place, you know."

"Reely? Well they certainly taught you well, Mr.—er . . ."

"Call me Ernest."

"I'm Doris. Well, I'm an actress reely and my professional name in France is Désirée. But I like Doris best. Oooh, what a lovely chassis!"

"Where are you performing currently, Doris?" asked Rowbotham, dipping and swaying to perfection, and she following him with liquid grace.

"We-e-e-l, I'm reely resting at the moment," said Doris, "but I played the role of the Rose Queen at the Folies in Menton last season. Tiring! You wouldn't believe! I had to wear this head-dress of roses that well nigh reached the ceiling. Mind you, I wasn't required to wear much else at the time." She giggled.

"I like you, Doris," said Rowbotham.

"I like you, too, Ernest," she responded. "Do you want to come back home with me?"

Rowbotham, now that he was faced with the reality of his mission, missed his footing and all but deposited the pair of them into the middle of Mr. Freddie et ses Boys, but recovered himself in time.

"Yes, I would like that very much, Doris," he said. "There is, however, a small complication . . ."

"Reely—what's that?"

"It's my Uncle Luigi. He will insist on coming. To—um—watch, you know."

"That's him over there, your Uncle Luigi, in the wheelchair?"

"Mmmm. He doesn't say much. He just—well—looks."

"Oh, the poor old dear. It's terrible when they go like that. How kind of you to take him around, Ernest. But where's the complication?"

"Well, I thought—well—him looking on and all, you might object."

Doris waved a shapely little hand and pouted. "Not me, ducks. Where's the harm in the poor old gentleman looking on? It's all Nature, innit?"

Rowbotham was touched and charmed by this evidence of so generous a heart, and went straight to inform Uncle Luigi that he had, so to speak, "clicked" with a genuine (presumably genuine) red-headed lady of the town who was, furthermore, palpably the best-looking female in the room.

(Except, perhaps, Miss Annabel Smith, when in *déshabillé?*)

Charles was summoned, and the four of them left the *salle de danse*. Miss Annabel Smith consulted her wrist-watch, jotted down the time in her notebook and followed after.

It was not till Rowbotham was seated in the back of the Duesenberg between Doris and Uncle Luigi, and, in catching her eye, was treated to what could only be described as a twinkle, that he fully realised the import of the enterprise to which he had set his hand. And he was afraid.

Doris's apartment was at the back of town, top floor of a prewar block that was served by a rickety lift suitable only for two persons, and that at a squeeze. Rowbotham and Doris went first; four floors at dead-slow speed, eye to eye, with her voluptuous bosom in close propinquity to his dove-grey-clad chest. He supposed that the correct form would have been to kiss her, or perhaps offer her some form of caress, but the memory of the previous and only time he had so indulged—and the retribution which had swiftly followed—made him stay his lips, and his hands.

They came at length to the fourth floor, and the lift returned to bring Charles and Uncle Luigi. There was a nagging doubt in the corner of Rowbotham's mind: a matter of protocol. He was about to express it; but Doris forestalled him immediately they got inside the sitting-room of her apartment, a sizeable chamber stuffed with overblown furniture and nick-nacks, with the centrepiece of an enormous chaise longue, or day-bed.

"I'm going to slip into something cosy, ducks," she said, squeezing his arm. "Just leave a thousand francs on the mantelpiece over there for little Doris, then we can just concentrate on enjoying ourselves, can't we?"

She kissed him lightly on the nose and went off into another room. Charles and his charge entered almost immediately afterwards, and Uncle Luigi having been established in the centre of the room (with a good view of the chaise longue), the dutiful chauffeur retired down to wait in the limousine.

"Right, you dirty old corpse," said Rowbotham, but without heat. "I hope you're going to enjoy what comes next, but I can tell you that I wish I were elsewhere. I wouldn't admit it to anyone but you, but I am scared silly."

From a wallet well stuffed with French currency with which he had been provided by his uncle's lawyers in London, Rowbotham took out a thousand-franc note and laid it on the chimney-piece as requested. What Doris referred to as the mantelpiece was so littered with photos and nick-nacks that there was scarcely room to lay a matchstick. He tucked the note under the arm of a doll in a crinoline.

And then his eye met—*it!* . . .

In the sudden joy and wonder, he scarcely heard Doris re-enter the room; only the reflected movement in the mirror above the chimney-piece alerted him, and that, because of his sudden euphoria, not quickly.

Presently, he turned. She had changed into a garment which, as Rowbotham knew from the contents of certain publications greatly esteemed by schoolboys which he had constantly been obliged to confiscate during his teaching days, was called—as he remembered—a camiknicker, and was constructed in a material so insubstantial as to permit one to establish that Doris was, if not a genuine redhead, at least one who pursued red-headedness determinedly.

But he had eyes only for her eyes, and sought to communicate the wonder that he had found, and perhaps to win back its echo from her.

He held out the photo that he had taken down from the chimney-piece—and it lovingly framed in a silver frame.

"This—this is one of the classic Great Western Railway Singlewheelers," he whispered in awed tones.

The wonder was echoing back! . . .

"She's the four-two-two Express Engine Number three-oh-four-six," breathed Doris.

"Not Number three-oh-four-six!" he cried. "Not Lord of the Isles!"

"Yes, reely!" said Doris. "Lord of the Isles. Me dad took the photo at Paddington station before the war, when him and me was there taking train numbers."

"You have train numbers?" asked Rowbotham. "Great Western Railway train numbers—dating from before the war?"

"Three whole books full."

"*Here*—in Monte Carlo?"

"Where else, Ernest? Wouldn't go anywhere without them."

"May I—*see* them?"

"Of course. I'll go get them."

While Miss Annabel Smith sat in the shade of a pine tree across the street and irritably glanced at her watch from time to time, while Charles the chauffeur lolled in the driving seat of the Duesenberg and eyed the passing girls, while Uncle

The Man Who Broke the Bank at Monte Carlo   65

Luigi gazed sightlessly at the unencumbered chaise longue, Doris and Ernest pored over the dog-eared notebooks that told the story of so much love and happiness.

5564   5701   1108   2848   4995 . . .

"Ah, those were the golden days," said he. "They don't make engines like that any more. Nothing's been the same, not since the war. Still, there's plenty of the old engines and rolling stock still around."

"You came down on the Blue Train, Ernest?"

"Mmmm. Engine Number three-one-eight-oh-one and Sleeping Car two-six-four-four-A."

"Do you mind if I write those numbers down?"

"Feel free, Doris," said Rowbotham. "D'you know, I've always adored the Great Western Railway, ever since I was a very small boy."

"There's no other like it," she replied, her eyes misting. "Me dad took me to Paddington every Sunday afternoon, carried me on his shoulders he did, all the way from Hackney, winter and summer. We used to sit in the train hall—"

"Built by Isambard Kingdom Brunel," interposed Rowbotham. "In 1844 by that genius of the G.W.R. So sorry to interrupt you, Doris."

"'Sorl right, Ernest. As I was saying, we used to sit there all the afternoon, taking down train numbers, and sometimes me dad would take a photo with his Kodak—if there was something special come in, like that old Singlewheeler."

"What times you must have had, Doris," said Rowbotham. "I, who lived in Worthing and was sent to boarding school in Rutland, seldom had the opportunity to visit Paddington, that Temple of the G.W.R., and had to do my train-number-taking on the less prestigious lines."

"It's not the same, is it?" said Doris. "I mean, sometimes when the weather was very bad, Dad and me'd not go any further than Hackney Wick station and see the London,

Midland and Scottish trains come through—but it wasn't the same. Not the same."

"Once, once only," said Rowbotham, "we went on holiday to Penzance, my parents and I."

"Not all the way to Penzance? Ooooh, Ernest!"

"From Paddington, right to the end of the line. Reading and Castle Cary, Exeter and Dawlish, with the engine smoke blowing out across the estuary of the river Exe as we steamed right by the water's edge at nearly a hundred miles an hour . . ."

"Oh, Ernest!" She seized hold of his hand. "Do go on!"

It was past six o'clock when they dragged themselves away from the delights of the Great Western Railway and into the world of reality in which they both inhabited. Doris indicated the chaise longue. "We never did, did we?" she said. "Would you like to? . . ."

"It's been so nice," he replied. "Let's leave it at that for today."

"I feel terrible about taking your money, Ernest," she said. "I feel as if I should be paying *you* for the pleasure you've given me this afternoon, I reely do."

"The pleasure's been mine, Doris," he said. And kissed her cheek.

"I hope your uncle's not been too bored," she said. "I expect he came here looking forward to fireworks, poor old chap."

Rowbotham chuckled. "Uncle didn't actually specify what he wanted to watch and hear," he said. "So he really can't complain—*can you, Uncle?*" he added loudly.

"Poor old gentleman, I think he's fast asleep," said Doris.

"Oh, he's right out of this world," said Rowbotham. "You wouldn't believe."

They took a tender farewell of each other, and she, who was sure that somewhere she had another print of Engine

Number 3046, promised to search it out and give it to him the next time they met—which, she added, she hoped would be soon.

Rowbotham himself handled Uncle Luigi and his chair down the shuddering, antique lift. Charles was dozing at the wheel of the Duesenberg when they got out. The sun was down. Miss Annabel Smith had moved out from under the shadow of the pine and was taking the last of the warmth on a park bench opposite. On an impulse, Rowbotham went over to speak to her.

"Sorry to have kept you waiting so long, Miss Smith," he said. "But you know how these things are. Time simply flies when one's enjoying oneself, don't you always find?"

Her eyes—he saw for the first time that there was a violet tinge to the blueness—blazed with anger. "I'm so glad that you found enjoyment!" she snapped, "because that"—and she pointed across to the apartment building—"will be your lot every Thursday afternoon—*for the rest of your life!*"

"How fortunate for me," said Rowbotham. "Good evening, Miss Smith."

He raised his panama hat to her and departed, leaving her glowering.

CHAPTER 6

A Farman air liner of Air France clawed its painful way into the sky above Le Bourget and headed south, twin engines clattering. The First Class compartment, which was differenced from second class by a plywood partition and a *haute cuisine* luncheon, was occupied by only four personages, who sat, in pairs facing, at each side of the narrow aisle. They comprised a lady of tremendous physical allure, whose uncertain age had been masked by several face-lifts and all the paraphernalia of the beauty parlour and the *coiffeur*; a dark man with a scarred cheek who sat facing her; and two other characters who, from their appearance, might have been retired prize-fighters—in any event, the sort of fellows over whom one might not wish to spill one's beer in a bar. All were dressed in the height of fashion, the lady in a mink coat and cloche hat, the men in well-cut suits and handmade shirts, handmade shoes of snakeskin and crocodile. All had the appearance of southern Italians—or Sicilians.

Following a series of alarming bumps as the aeroplane passed over the hot, reeking chimneys of the outer suburbs, the woman broke the silence:

"It is my considered opinion," she said, "that the thing which this English guy Rowbotham is trundling around is not the corpse of Luigi Gaudi, but a stuffed dummy. And Luigi Gaudi is just waiting around in his wheelchair—alive—till the heat is off and he can make his collect. Am I not right, Larry?"

The man she addressed as Larry, the scarfaced one sitting opposite her, hunched his shoulders and spread his hands.

"For five and a half, call it six million bucks, anything could happen," he said. "Maybe you're right, Liza. For six million, Luigi might make play to outsmart Mr. Death himself. All I know is, Weinberg the mortician on Greener Street took possession of Luigi's corpse January third last and embalmed same as per instructions. All this me and the boys checked out. Right, fellers?" This addressed to the two fearsome-looking creatures across the gangway.

"Sure thing, Larry," testified one.

"We got the truth out of that Weinberg real good, did we not, Aldo?"

"Absolutely," averred his companion. "Poeta here used the pincers and Weinberg sang like a bird at the sight of them."

"And he still stuck to the story," declared Poeta. "After I had took out all the fingernails of his left hand, he would have ratted on his own beloved mother had she been alive. But right to the end he gave it to us thus—he embalmed the dead body of Luigi Gaudi, and he did it real good."

Larry spread his hands again, addressing the woman. "So, Liza, unless someone worked a switch, this is still the stuffed corpse of Luigi we are after. And the English guy, his nephew."

Liza stared out of the window savagely, down at the railway line a thousand feet below, along which the air liners navigated to the Midi. There was a train below: the Blue Train. On the long straights, it perceptibly drew ahead of the aeroplane.

"You should have killed him that day, Larry!" she whispered, and her voice was choked with bitterness. "You should have rubbed him out, like I explained you."

The scarfaced man spread his hands. "I gave him a whole

burst, Liza," he protested. "The rat just had the lucky breaks, that's all. I stood in the doorway, didn't I, fellers? . . ."

"That's right, that's right, Larry," chorused the other pair.

"And I sprayed the rat as he sat there at his special place at his special table in Pauli's. He went over, gushing blood like he was a fire-plug. Right, boys?"

"Right, right, Larry."

Liza took from her crocodile handbag a lace handkerchief and dabbed a tear from each false-lashed, mascaraed eye. "He killed my man," she said brokenly. "He killed my Francesco. For that he should have died that day."

"Sure, sure, Liza," said Larry, reaching out to pat her free hand. "But he just had the breaks."

"Luigi in a wheelchair has been as much trouble to me as Luigi on his feet."

"You do great, Liza," said Larry. "You run the mob with the same great style as Francesco did when he was around."

The reassurance appeared to harden the woman's resolve immediately. She put away her handkerchief. The dark eyes glittered determination of the kind that the lioness displays when hunting at a water-hole while her mate lies snoozing in the shade of a banyan tree.

"He sent me Francesco's ears," she said. "That and the dirty poem. For that, I'm going to lay my hands on everything he's got, alive or dead." She sat back, she was all businesslike now. "Listen, we know that three weeks before he died—or was supposed to have died—Luigi bought up between five and a half and six million dollars' worth of high grade uncut diamonds. For what? Was he maybe going to take them with him, to bribe Saint Peter at the Pearly Gates for admission?"

"They were maybe for the Limey nephew," ventured Larry. "Luigi never had no time for banks, save as places to heist."

Their discourse was interrupted by the arrival, down the

narrow, swaying gangway, of a typical French waiter in long apron, wing-collar, patent leather hair. Following him were two sprightly lassies in frilly aprons and caps, who were eyed with some favour by Aldo and Poeta. Luncheon was being served. The menu may not have rivalled that of the Blue Train, still steaming below them, but it was by no means inconsiderable:

> Hors-d'oeuvre
> Langouste Parisienne
> Poulet Sauté Chasseur
> Jambon d'York à la Gelée
> Salade Niçoise
> Glace Plombière
> Fromages
> Corbeille de Fruits

"I'm going to lay my hands on those rocks," said Liza, stabbing at a truffled mussel. "Somebody's going to talk. Either Luigi, if he's still alive, or that nephew."

"I brought the pincers, Liza," declared Poeta, leering.

About the time that Liza Carlos and her minions were tackling their York ham in aspic, Ernest Rowbotham was pushing his Uncle Luigi along the boulevard. He was under no instructions to do so; this was merely a bonus for the deceased: a pleasant outing in the sun and shade. Both wore identical white silk suits. Uncle still retained his wide-brimmed and sinister-looking hat, but Rowbotham sported his old school boater, banded with the colours of the First Cricket XI and worn jauntily, à la Maurice Chevalier.

The *bon ton* of Monte Carlo was out in the boulevard, strolling or partaking of pre- or post-prandial drinks at the pavement cafes under the lime trees and the palms. As they slowly progressed (for the essence of playing the *boulevardier* is to remain in view of, and keep in sight, as many people as possible at any one time), Rowbotham kept his uncle *au fait* with the passing sights and the charivari.

"There's an orchestra in the bandstand in the square in front of the Casino, Uncle," he said. "They're playing selections from *The Merry Widow*. There are yachts out in the bay, big ones. The sea is very blue—the way a child would colour it, straight out of his paintbox without diluting or mixing the pigment.

"Now we come to a cafe. I think a little later we'll stop and have a drink, but not here, I fancy. There sit Messrs. Diaghilev, Lifar and Cocteau, who were witnesses to that ghastly scene on the train when the detective took off your mask and revealed your awful phiz—" he shuddered "—and they're staring at us rather narrowly, so we'll move on.

"Don't look now! Here comes that chap Selfridge with the two colourful ladies, one on each arm. I wonder how he copes with two when I couldn't even . . . Oh, my God, what are they going to do when they clap eyes on you again? Faint at the sight, I shouldn't wonder, and make a most dreadful scene out here in front of everybody! I think I'll turn around, stop and pretend to be looking out across the bay. Tum-te-upty-tum-tum. Mmmm—they've gone. That was a narrow shave. Honestly—the trouble you cause me, Uncle!"

They progressed. The sound of the orchestra in the bandstand faded into the background and was taken over by the strains of a three-piece ensemble in a palm-shrouded cafe playing "Tales from the Vienna Woods." At the third rank of tables set back from the pavement sat an elegant figure in a canary yellow silk suit and panama hat whom Rowbotham immediately recognised as his friend of the Casino, the helpful Mr. Ezekiel Bragg. His first inclination was to go and join him, but Bragg's table was sandwiched in rather too densely for him to negotiate the wheelchair without causing the most awful upheaval, and anyhow Bragg was busy writing postcards, his head bent over the task, clearly unaware of his presence. Best leave the renewing of their acquaintance till the next time, thought Rowbotham, and walked on.

He had gone perhaps half a block, and was abreast of a dress shop whose elegance and exclusivity was announced by an enormous window occupied only by one simple little black frock, and had just passed a large black saloon car parked by the kerb, when there came a footfall behind him, and an importuning voice:

"Got a light, bud?"

He turned to regard the largest and most frightful-looking man he had ever set eyes upon.

"I—I'm sorry, but I don't smoke," he responded. Really, the chap looked more like a gorilla than a human. The front hairline was in so close a proximity to the eyebrows as almost to be married.

"Ged in da car, bud!" growled the other.

"I . . ." faltered Rowbotham.

"You heard me, bud—ged in da car. Unless you would like I should twist your head around so dat it still faces front after circling on your neck a coupla times."

"But—I can't leave my—my friend here . . ."

"Dat guy won't come to no harm, as we both know well. Ged in da car!"

The car door, the rear door, was open. Rowbotham obeyed—there seeming to be no alternative but to be garrotted in plain view; and surely no passer-by, however public-spirited, was going to raise a finger against, nor make the slightest protest to, his executioner presumptive.

The door slammed on him. He found that he was seated beside a sharp-featured man who sucked at a large cigar. The giant had taken his place on the other side, sandwiching him. There were two more men up front. As the car drew away, he cast a worried glance back through the rear window. Uncle Luigi remained where he had left him, seated in his wheelchair, gazing sightlessly ahead down the sunlit boulevard, the subject of very little attention from the dazzling crowds who sauntered past.

"Don't you worry about Luigi Gaudi, Mr. Rowbotham," said the man on his left, the sharp-featured one. "Luigi was a pretty fast mover in the old days before he took to the wheelchair. But he won't be moving anyplace today. He'll be there when you get back—*if* you get back." His chuckle was echoed by the other three.

Rowbotham was filled with a sudden dread. "Where—where are you taking me?" he breathed.

"We're taking you for a ride," responded the other. "And you can call me Nicky."

"But, I don't want to go for a ride," said Rowbotham with as much firmness as he could muster, and it was not a lot. "Why should I wish to go for a ride with a group of perfect strangers?"

"We are far from perfect, Mr. Rowbotham," responded Nicky—a sally which won him another guffaw from his friends.

"Besides," said Rowbotham, with a flash of improvisation, "I'm prone to car sickness, which is why I travel everywhere by train."

For some reason that Rowbotham could not fathom, this *non sequitur* reduced his unwanted companions to a state of most extreme mirth, and the driver—a creature whom his colleagues addressed as Abie—was so assaulted by a paroxysm of laughter that he bid fair to swerve the car and drive it off the coast road and over the cliff into the sea, a feat that won him a sharp reprimand from the man, Nicky, who was quite clearly in charge.

They took him to a lay-by off the cliff road: a miniature canyon carved into the rock face opposite the dazzling blueness of the sea, a quiet arbour set about with whispering cypresses, a haven of peace and a balm for the uneasy soul.

Given Rowbotham's present circumstances and his companions, the place offered no balm at all.

"Okay, Mr. Rowbotham," said Nicky, when they had all got out. "Back up against that tree and we'll have us a little talk."

"What—are we going to talk about?" whispered Rowbotham, wishing that he had not lost control over his voice, and conscious that his nether lip was trembling.

"Don't stall, Mr. Rowbotham," said Nicky, with a sorrowful note to his voice. "When you stall like that, it grieves my heart to think that we shall maybe be here all day. And that will be painful."

"Supposing you—you gave me a lead?" suggested Rowbotham.

The other shrugged. "Okay, I'm a reasonable guy—save when roused. For a lead: how much did Luigi Gaudi leave you, the rat?"

Rowbotham swallowed hard. "Um—six million dollars."

The other beamed, turned to his associates: they were beaming also. "So, we're getting someplace," he said. "And we're moving fast. I pose another question, Mr. Rowbotham."

"Feel free," replied Rowbotham.

"Call me Nicky," beamed the other.

"Yes, of course. Please continue—er—Nicky."

"Where is the loot stashed?"

"Come again?"

Nicky sighed. "Suddenly this dialogue has become bogged down. I will attempt to make myself more clear. In what sanctuary are these greenbacks secreted? Name the haven where Luigi's lettuce is ensconced. WHERE IS THE MONEY

HID OUT?" he ended in a shout that echoed around the little canyon like a dried pea in a spinning bucket.

"Well." Rowbotham thought for a few moments. "You would scarcely believe this . . ."

"Try it on me for size."

"I really don't know. I don't know where the money is. My uncle's lawyers provided me with pocket money—ample—for this trip. Apart from that everything's been paid for in advance: the hotel charges, money to play with in the Casino—everything."

Nicky nodded impatiently. "Okay, okay, we are talking about peanuts," he said. "Where is the main part of the spondulicks?"

"Why, in a bank account, I suppose," said Rowbotham. "But I never thought to enquire where, for, as I have explained, I simply have not had the need to draw any."

His captors looked at him long and hard, and then at each other.

"Boys," said Nicky, "what we have here is a pseudologist, a teller of tales. I had great hopes for Mr. Rowbotham, but I have been disappointed."

"I'm telling you the truth!" declared Rowbotham. "That money must be in a bank somewhere, but I simply don't know where."

The other sighed and took the lapel of Rowbotham's silk jacket tenderly between finger and thumb. He spoke quietly, without heat: "I can believe that Luigi would have put his kid sister into a whore-house," he said. "With no great exercise of credulity, I would likewise accept that he would—the cemetery authorities being willing—have grown tomatoes on his mother's grave. But, for reasons I will not trouble you with, I know that Luigi Gaudi would never have put a single nickel into any bank." He concluded his peroration by ripping the lapel—viciously—revealing the beautiful, hand-sewn

Savile Row underpinnings of the garment. "So talk, Mr. Rowbotham—AND TALK FAST!"

"I–I . . ." To his dismay, Rowbotham saw them close about him, the hideous giant, the tall thin man with the wall-eye, the grinning one with the badly fitting false teeth. "I don't know!" he concluded lamely.

"Make with a little persuasion, Boris," said Nicky. "Seize hold of Mr. Rowbotham, Elephant, so that Boris can get to work without fear of interruption. When Boris has finished with you, Mr. Rowbotham—assuming that you do not sing for us this afternoon—you'll be able to go back and sing boy soprano."

Rowbotham shrank back against the tree. Grinning, Boris was already fumbling with the waistband of the white silk suit—*his* suit, and the creature called Elephant was reaching out to pinion him. With a cry of alarm, he ducked aside and ran—ran like a hare, and he had been a good track runner in his boyhood—for the exit from the canyon.

The tall gangster pulled out a pistol and aimed it at the fleeing figure; Nicky knocked the weapon up with a snarl.

"You want to throw away our meal-ticket, you bum?" he grated. "Get after him, and I'll bring the automobile. He can't get far."

Rowbotham swung left out of the canyon, left towards Monte Carlo, and going fine. In his youth, his asthma notwithstanding, he had been a capable middle-distance runner, holding the school record for some years with a time for the half mile which was well under three minutes. On this particular afternoon, with the brilliant Mediterranean on his right, the craggy cliff on his left, the pounding of footfalls behind him and a dread fear of reverting to boy soprano, he gave of his all.

The tarmac beneath his feet was soggy from the intense sun; it formed a heat haze ahead, blurring the cliff edge, shimmering the horizon of sea and the white sails of yachts. It made for heavy going.

All too soon, alas, his breath became laboured. God, if only I'd stayed fit, he told himself. If only I'd given up smoking in my twenties. If only I'd lived a cleaner life, with cold baths in the morning and all that stuff. If only—

Clearly, above the drumming in his ears, he heard the sound of a car engine. In addition to the runners, they were now bringing their transport into play.

No way of escape. To the right, a sheer drop to the sea that curled and foamed among the craggy rocks; on his left, the smooth, unscaleable cliff; ahead, the ribbon of tarmac along which his plodding feet were travelling at an ever-decreasing pace.

The sound of the motor snarled nearer, drowning all else. He had the thought that maybe they intended to run him over, to silence him for ever, since they could wrest no secret from him. Yes, they were coming right up behind him. He swerved in his flight—and fell headlong onto the tarmac.

The car screeched to a halt beside him.

"Get up, get up, you fool!" A female voice, very bossy. He looked up to see Miss Annabel Smith glaring at him over the coming of an exceedingly snappy little open sports car, a Bugatti. "Get up, unless you want to be caught again."

She gestured behind her. A hundred yards away, three running figures were strung out, but coming on strongly. And the black saloon had just pulled out of the canyon. Rowbotham leapt to his feet as if the road had turned into a red-hot griddle, and clambered in beside Miss Smith. She snicked off the hand-brake, let out the clutch. The little car screeched away, plastering six months' wear of tyre rubber on the tarmac in its take-off.

"I saw them pick you up," she shouted above the din of the acceleration. "I was right behind you when that torpedo bundled you into the black automobile. By the time I found myself some transport, you were way out of sight along the cliff road. I went on through to Menton before it dawned on me that they must have turned off someplace. So I came back. Just in time, it seems." She glanced into the rear-view mirror. "The black automobile's following behind and doing its best, but it will never catch up with this baby." She depressed her foot, and the Bugatti took the next sharp bend in a power slide. Rowbotham braced himself, took hold of everything in sight. Miraculously, the car straightened up at the completion of the turn, gave a little jink to right and left and sped on, gathering revs all the way down the last, descending slope to Monte Carlo.

"What did those guys back there want with you?" she shouted.

"They're after my legacy," he shouted in reply.

"That figures. The Chicago gangland's run on a strict basis of rationing territories as between one mob and another. Luigi Gaudi was no respecter of territories, and I've no doubt your friends consider that your legacy—or a very large part of it—is rightfully theirs."

"It's not a pleasant prospect for me, Miss Smith."

"I'm worried for you. This, however, is not to be compared with the way I'd feel if it was the Carlos mob who were after you."

"Why's that, Miss Smith?"

"It was the killing of Francesco Carlos that led to the retaliation which brought Luigi Gaudi to his wheelchair. His widow, Liza, never got over Francesco's death. She took charge of the operation and runs it with a rod of iron. The slightest deviation from the code and she orders an execution. There must be enough people standing around in concrete boots at the bottom of Lake Michigan—and I speak of those put there on Liza Carlos's orders—to fill a fair-sized movie theatre. They call her the Concrete Widow."

"I'm glad she hasn't got wind of my legacy, Miss Smith. I don't suppose she'd view me with any great regard—considering I'm Luigi Gaudi's nephew."

"Just keep hoping, Mr. Rowbotham. Just keep hoping."

The bare road gave way to an avenue lined with palms and *bijou* villas where lawns were sprinkled and lawn-mowers whirred in counterpoint to the chirruping of the cicadas in the herbaceous borders.

"I'm rather worried about Uncle," said Rowbotham. "Having to leave him like that, right out in the busy street. I hope no one's taken him."

"*Who* would take him?" she retorted. "With all the handsome men and pretty women around in Monte Carlo, who'd have designs on a badly processed corpse?"

"I suppose you're right," said Rowbotham. "Still—I shall feel happier when I've got him back. I know he's only a dirty-minded old corpse, but, oddly, I've come to grow quite fond of him, and regard him as a surrogate living person. The way —it sounds absurd I know—I used to feel about my teddy bear."

"I will return this car to its rightful owner," said Miss Smith, "and then we together will go and recover your uncle."

"You didn't—*steal*—this marvellous Bugatti?" asked he in tones of awe.

"Borrowed," she replied. "Some rich playboy left it parked right outside the Casino with the keys and all. With any luck, he'll never know it went away for a while. And all he's lost is a few litres of gasoline—for which I will put a hundred-franc note in the glove compartment—so."

"You are scrupulously honest, Miss Smith," said Rowbotham, with no attempt at irony.

Miss Annabel Smith's probity was well rewarded. No hue and cry awaited them when she slid the Bugatti into the space from whence she had taken it outside the Casino. They walked quietly away, and no one called after them.

It was then that the luck ran out. It was mid-afternoon, and the well-heeled visitors were taking their siesta, to reinforce themselves for another late night on the gaming tables, or other sportive pursuits. A few high-stepping gigolos were promenading and a handful of cocottes oscillated and jiggled, all on the look-out for whom they might devour.

But outside the high-toned dress shop, there was no sign of the forlorn figure in the wheelchair.

CHAPTER 7

"Perhaps your chauffeur happened by, saw him and took him back to the Paris," suggested Annabel Smith.

Rowbotham shook his head. "I gave Charles the day off. He drove the Duesenberg to Grasse to see his mother. I've lost Uncle. He's gone. And I suppose that that qualifies me for the loss of my inheritance to your dogs' home."

"Not necessarily," she said. "Frankly, the terms of the will, though generally a disaster for you, take absolutely no account of your actually *losing* the corpse. I shouldn't be telling you this, but any competent lawyer you consulted would so advise you."

"Nevertheless, it's kind of you to make the point," he said.

"Think nothing of it."

They were seated at a table in a sidewalk cafe. She was sipping lemon tea, he a large *fine*. They had repaired there to discuss the situation.

"Do I go to the police?" he asked.

"I think at this stage that it would be precipitate," replied Miss Smith. "After all, in the terms of the will—and if you want to retain the legacy—you are stuck with Monte Carlo for life. The police will not like this situation at all. The local authorities, who govern the Casino and the various amenities for rich visitors upon whom the livelihood of the Principality depends, will not take kindly to the notion of some guy pushing a stuffed corpse around the high spots, and I would say that the longer you keep this information from them the better."

"You're right, of course," said Rowbotham. "I mean, for instance, if Uncle and I were banned from the Casino, might I not be deemed to have defaulted on his instructions?"

"You might well," she conceded. "And you may be sure that the Universal Dogs' Home of Cincinnati would pursue the matter through the courts with the utmost vigour."

"Again, thanks for your advice, Miss Smith," said Rowbotham. "You have been most helpful in my time of trouble."

"You made an awful mess of that lovely suit coat," she said. "When we get back to the hotel, let me have it and I'll sew up the lapel again."

"Oh, please don't bother. I've plenty more suits."

"No, you give it to me. I hate waste. My father taught me to hate waste, but to enjoy the occasional extravagance. Do you know the difference between extravagance and waste, Mr. Rowbotham?"

"I can't say that I do, Miss Smith. Tell me."

"Extravagance is a two-dollar cigar. Waste is to light it with a dollar bill. That was my father's definition. He was something of a homespun philosopher, and he arrived at all his own conclusions. What are you drinking?"

"This is a liqueur brandy," said Rowbotham.

"Something I have never tried," said Miss Smith. "I think I should like to try one. And then we must address ourselves to ideas for recovering your uncle."

Two *fines* later, and a third one on order—*they* came . . .

Jolly bouncing boys, joshing each other along the pavement and stamping in the gutter, where the street-cleaners had released a small torrent of water to wash away the silt of dust and sand. They were barefoot, looked like fishermen's kids— which, indeed, they were.

"I have the most original idea!" exclaimed Rowbotham. "Boys are the same the world over, and these look no different. They know the streets, the ins and outs of people's ways, they spot anything unusual that's happening in their open-air bailiwick. Let's use them to seek out and find Uncle, if they can."

"That suggestion has the touch of brilliance," declared Annabel Smith, who found to her surprise that she was having difficulty in articulating the word "suggestion."

"*Venez ici, mes garçons,*" called Rowbotham. "*Nous verrons de parlez avec vous dans un—a—un* particular matter..."

"Suppose you let me handle this, Ernest," said Annabel (they had slipped into first-name terms after the second *fine*), laying a gentle hand on his arm and dispelling, by the gesture and a smiling glance, any suggestion that his approach to the boys had been inadequate. "I speak the local patois, you see."

"Ah, the patois is very important," said Rowbotham, grateful for the elegant get-out she had offered him.

She addressed the boys in rapid French, of which they clearly understood every word, for they nodded and grinned delightedly. What she expounded—as Rowbotham was able imperfectly to understand—was that the boys should split up, some of them going one way, some the other (pointing), search for an old gentleman in a wheelchair and bring him back here. She did not state that the old gentleman was dead, but indicated that he might be asleep. And the reward for finding him—she placed the note on the table and anchored it with an ashtray—was ten francs. The boys departed, whooping with high delight.

"You handled that jolly well, Annabel," said Rowbotham. "To tell you the truth, I'm not much of a linguist. I read Geography at Cambridge. Ah, here comes the waiter with the bottle. We've made fair inroads into that bottle, and I confess

I feel quite squiffed. What do you do with yourself when you're not working for the Dogs' Home, Annabel?"

A very handsome Rolls-Royce sailed past them: chauffeur and footman up front, a lady in a picture hat in the back, a Pekinese dog glowering at the passing scene through the window. And now the harbour was full of the white and coloured sails of yachts returning from their afternoon cruise. Despite his predicament, Rowbotham felt a curious sense of well-being.

"I travel, mostly," she said. "Last year, I went to Hollywood for a vacation, where my Cousin Lily works as a secretary in one of the big studios. The best part was the train journey."

"You like trains?" His response was immediate and excited.

"Why, yes," she said. "They're so convenient and comfortable. I hate flying because it's so scary, and anyhow, I'm never in any great hurry. What's that quote from Robert Louis Stevenson?"

"'To travel hopefully is a better thing than to arrive,'" supplied Rowbotham. "I think we may have a very great deal in common, Miss Smith—I mean, Annabel. Have you ever heard of the Great Western Railway of England?"

"No, I have not, Ernest," she responded, her firm chin in her shapely, small hand, her dark eyes fixed upon him, their brilliance only slightly obfuscated by the thick lenses of her glasses. "Tell me all about the Great Western Railway of England."

And he did.

Commissaire Paul Darré, having resigned himself to the prospect of a ninth offspring, had sought to augment his income to accommodate the putative arrival. This he did by applying to the Département for permission to sit for the higher Civil Service examination, which, if passed, would fit him for a higher grade and a commensurate salary. Being a resident of Monte Carlo, he also—literally—hedged his bet by trying out (strictly academically) a series of systems he had cobbled together to beat the roulette table. He was working on this, using a miniature wheel and a ball the size of a pea and a well-stuffed notebook as thick as a Bible, when his assistant Martin entered precipitately.

"Can't you learn to knock?" demanded Darré, irritably, striking off an imaginary fifty thousand francs' winnings which he had lost after the pea-sized ball had, against all the Laws of Probability as Darré imperfectly understood them, landed six consecutive times in a black receptacle.

"Sorry, Chief," responded his aide. "But I just had this wire from Interpol H.Q. in Vienna, which may shed some light on the Orange-road murders."

Darré pulled a long lip and, putting the little roulette wheel back in its drawer, locked it in there, along with his notebook.

"Continue," he growled.

"A party of four Americans arrived at Nice airport this afternoon," said Martin. "Following upon the double murder with Chicago-type gangster weapons, I have ordered a special, searching enquiry into United States visitors arriving in Monte Carlo from today."

"Very commendable," said Darré, thinking how profitable it would have been if the run of six blacks could have been translated to six reds in succession. He started working on the arithmetic . . .

"On the afternoon Air France plane from Paris today," said Martin, "there arrived"—he consulted his notebook—"a Mrs. Liza Carlos, and three men named Lawrence J. Rattazini, Aldo Ricasoli and Poeta Minghetti."

"You say they arrived in the Midi this afternoon, Martin?"

"That is so, Chief. Interpol informs us that they arrived in

Le Havre aboard the *Berengaria* on the fifteenth, travelled to Paris by rail and embarked upon the Air France flight shortly before noon today."

"And? . . ." Darré, who was used to, and generally tolerant of, his assistant's *longueurs*, wished on this occasion that he would come swiftly to the point (My God, he thought. If it had happened in reality: to have lost fifty thousand at the very *commencement* of the game! One would have had to take a second mortgage on the apartment, sell the automobile . . .).

"In short," said Martin, as if in answer to his Chief's unspoken plea, "these people are Chicago gangsters, and the woman Carlos is their ringleader, having taken over command upon the killing of her husband in a gangland feud."

Darré was all attention now, thoughts of his personal problems thrust aside by the call of duty. "What are they doing in Monte Carlo?—and I presume your interest lies in the fact that they came here from Nice."

Martin nodded. "They have checked in at the Paris. The purpose of their visit—they were questioned at the airport upon my instigation, and also searched—is—quote—recreational."

"Weapons?"

"No weapons, Chief. Apart from their baggage, which was gone through with great diligence, they had a small wooden crate containing books and other items. This had been cleared by Customs at Le Havre along with the rest."

Darré rubbed his chin—the stubbly bit which his razor had missed that morning. "Do Chicago gangsters require so much reading material?" he asked. "And what were the 'other items,' so called?"

Martin consulted his notebook.

"There is a croquet set," he said. "Hoops, balls, mallets—so called."

"Curious," commented Darré. "If this is the 'recreation' in question, why come all the way to Monte Carlo to play croquet when they could just as easily play it in Chicago? Anything else?"

"A train set, Chief."

"Did you say a *train* set?"

"A model train set. Of the Blue Train."

"That I find extremely odd, and inexplicable—unless it is a present for a young relation or friend living in Monte Carlo."

Martin sniffed. "Not necessarily, Chief," he said. "There are men—grown men—who are deeply interested in model trains. And other models."

Darré hunched his shoulders. "I suppose you're right," he conceded. "It is not out of the question that a Chicago gangster could also be a retarded adolescent."

He could have bitten off his tongue as soon as he said it—suddenly remembering that Martin sailed his model yacht on the round pond in the Casino gardens most Sunday afternoons.

At the end of four *fines,* Rowbotham had given Annabel Smith a comprehensive outline of the history and excellence of the Great Western Railway, Isambard Kingdom Brunel—its guiding genius—and all. She, for her part, had listened to his discourse without interruption save to pose occasional and —in his opinion—extremely intelligent questions. When he had done, they both had another fill-up of their glasses.

"Annabel," said Rowbotham, studying her, his head on one side, deliberating. "There is something I've been wanting to ask you—and I hope you won't take it amiss."

"We shall have to see about that," she responded coolly. "Why don't you try me, Ernest?"

"Well, it's the way you look," he began, and made a general gesture that encompassed her extremely unbecoming hair-style; the uncompromising spectacles; total lack of rouge, face-powder, kohl; the gunny-sack frock; the cloche hat unembellished by so much as a flower or a bunch of cherries.

"You don't like the way I look?" she asked, and without a hint of tartness. "But you haven't been *invited* to admire me."

It was a response that would have reduced Rowbotham—in normal circumstances, *vis-à-vis* a member of the gentle sex—to impotent silence; but this was not a normal circumstance for him to deal with; he was fortified by half a bottle of champagne brandy, he was warmly aware that he had amused and interested her with his peroration upon the Great Western Railway; he also felt—and this impression was more subtle, more difficult to lay his finger on—that her response, far from being dismissive, was—not to put too fine a point on it—coquettish.

"I haven't offered you insult," he said. "And I don't believe that you are taking my comment amiss, because you know that I've seen you"—again the general gesture that took in her appearance—"without all that flimflam, and you know that I know that you are an extraordinarily beautiful woman. So—" he took a deep breath "—why do you get yourself up to be a fright?"

And then, to his horror, he saw that he had made her cry. She fumbled in her bag for a handkerchief, and not finding one was grateful for his offer of the silk show-piece from his breast pocket.

She sniffed and blinked tears for a while, and then she said: "I don't ever want to get involved with a man again. Not ever. And on this assignment—travelling to Europe all on my own (and would you believe that the captain of the liner I came across on tried to force his way into my cabin one night?)—I've opted out of being a woman any man would look at twice, so I bought these clothes in Le Havre and fixed myself up to match."

"Tell me all about it," said Rowbotham.

"Do you really want to hear?"

"I told you all about the Great Western and I. K. Brunel," he countered. "And you listened with interest."

So she told him.

It concerned a man: a personable, polo-playing charmer who did something in Wall Street that seldom interfered with his social commitments, which were both varied and considerable. Annabel met him at her cousin's wedding shortly after she had graduated from law school. Charmer Harold Forster was squiring a pretty redhead but seemed to find no difficulty in detaching himself from the latter enchantress and attaching himself to Annabel. They talked of this and that: how she had suffered the bereavement of her widowed father, an archetypal barefoot boy who had made a considerable fortune in oil, how she was hoping to set herself up in a law practice—that kind of thing. Harold Forster concentrated not upon the practicalities of his life and status, but upon more romantic texts: how, for instance, he had served in France as a member of the Lafayette Squadron and how, when it was all over, his Spad had been sprinkled with eleven black crosses to denote the "Huns" he had downed. And he spoke long and excitingly about polo, about racing J-class yachts, riding to hounds in the English shires with the Quorn and the Pytchley, drinking whisky and swapping jokes with the Prince of Wales—that kind of thing. By the end of the dinner that followed the wedding, Annabel was totally besotted with Harold Forster, who seemed to her to encapsulate all the manly virtues of Sir Galahad, Sir Lancelot of the Lake, Babe Ruth and Charles A. Lindbergh.

They were married in the fall of that year. Quietly, with only two witnesses, whom they more or less picked up out in the street by the city hall. No Niagara honeymoon for them, which Harold Forster declared to be bourgeois; they went to Havana, which—as Harold explained—was tremendously smart and much favoured by the English, who arrived by the ton in their de luxe cruise-liners. Harold was a confirmed Anglophile, particularly those of title.

They took the honeymoon suite in the old and elegant Hotel Habana, which overlooked the quiet parkland of the Campo de Marte. Besotted, the young bride unquestioningly gave her groom one of her cheque-books, every cheque signed blank, because, as he tried to explain before she silenced his mouth with kisses, he had left his behind.

That night—the first night of their honeymoon proper, since Harold Forster's many accomplishments did not include that of being a good sailor, and the sea voyage had been so rough as to preclude him from amorous dalliance at that time—Annabel fondly shooed her groom down to the cocktail bar, to await her while she fixed her hair and her face; which being done, she laid out her black lace night-dress and palpitated slightly. Then, slinkily gowned in a sequinned sheath, diamond solitaire engagement ring winking ostentatiously beside the plain gold band, she descended to join her beloved for dinner.

The brief scene that followed, in the cocktail bar, would have done justice to Greek tragedy. At stage centre was Harold Forster, seated at the bar, a large whisky sour in hand. Annabel entered stage right and tiptoed up to her beloved with the intent of placing her silk-gloved hands over his eyes and saying, "Guess who?" She was outdistanced, however, by a male character who advanced from stage left and, espying the elegant figure at the bar, immediately recognised him and greeted him thus:

"Hello, Harold, you old rake. How's that pretty wife of yours? How's Francine, hey?"

"There isn't much more to tell," she said. "I started back home that same night and cried all the way. I didn't even pack my honeymoon trousseau, but left it behind in Havana. Took only what I could cram into a hold-all and flew to Florida."

"He was already married," said Rowbotham, who had been listening to her story with respectful silence. "How awful for you."

"But not to Francine, I hasten to add." She took a long pull at her *fine*. "Francine was not even the previous attachment, but the one before that. He had a wife someplace, but I told my lawyers not to bother to search her out. They unearthed at least four other bigamous marriages. All of them to well-heeled dames with handy bank accounts. He didn't get a lot out of me and what it cost me, I reckon, was money well spent to be rid of him." She sighed. "I did take it somewhat amiss when I had the bill for my solitaire diamond engagement ring," she added.

"I'm so sorry," said Rowbotham.

"I learned my lesson," she said. "Men are fundamentally rotten. Handsome Harold Forster, the captain of that liner and maybe even you, Mr. Innocent Rowbotham—even though the five-hundred-page dossier we have on you at the Universal Dogs' Home of Cincinnati suggests that your life has been blameless so far. All I can say is—" she hiccuped "—all I can say is that no blameless and innocent guy would get a dame screw-eyed with booze on a sunny afternoon in Monte Carlo!"

And then, the first of the boys returned . . .

Four of them: laughing and joshing, stamping the gutter water, hopping from one foot to another, prancing; and one of them was pushing a wheelchair bearing a hunched figure in a large hat—more accurately, he was advancing by means of S-bends and sudden circles, simulating the effect, to the person in the wheelchair, of a scenic railway or a roller-coaster. The person in the wheelchair made no protest.

"M'sieu—mam'selle—we 'ave found 'eem!"

"Oh, dear me," said Rowbotham, rising. "What have we done, what *have* we done?"

Gingerly, he raised the hat of the figure in the chair, revealing the white-maned head of an extremely elderly gentleman with white moustache and beard. Fast asleep. Snoring happily.

"Annabel, would you please tell them that this isn't the old gentleman we are seeking, and will they take him back to where they found him, and they can have the ten francs, but please will they go on their merry way and forget the whole thing?" he pleaded.

Annabel complied. The boys returned the way they had come, rejoicing at their easy fortune, still stamping the gutter, still laughing and joshing; and the old sleeper in the wheelchair—whoever *he* was—continued to have the advantage of a roller-coaster effect.

"That was not a good idea of mine, after all," confessed Rowbotham.

She shook her head. "I have an idea it was not," she said.

Soon after, the second half of the posse advanced from the other direction. They came more circumspectly: no laughing and joshing, no puddle-stamping; they advanced as if a funeral cortège, nervously, with drawn young faces, eyeing each other, ready to run. As well they might: the incumbent of the wheelchair which one of them was pushing (at arms' length, gingerly, as if the handle was red hot), was regaling them—in English—in the foulest and filthiest terms that Rowbotham, who had not had the supreme advantage of serving in His Majesty's forces during the Great War, had ever encountered in all his days, even in the lower purlieus of private education.

"*M'sieu—mam'selle—regardez!*" The note lacked a little in triumphant overtones; there was mostly relief, as the boys unburdened themselves of their prize.

"Damn you, sir!" cried the figure in the wheelchair, a little man with a clipped moustache, poached egg eyes, yellowed teeth, albeit his own, and one leg, "do you know these young bounders?"

"No," lied Rowbotham. "But I think I can help you."

"That's damnably civil of you, sir," responded the other. And, seeing Annabel, smoothed his moustache and fixed her with a toothy grin. "Your servant, ma'am. The name's Jaggers. Colonel Harry Jaggers, late of the Royal Artillery."

But Annabel had taken aboard enough champagne brandy not to be bamboozled by military smoothness suddenly turned on.

"You disgusting old man!" she cried. "Give the boys ten francs, Ernest, and I'll tell them to take him and his dirty tongue back to where they found him!"

There remained nothing, then, but to find Uncle Luigi themselves. Accordingly, they drained their glasses, Rowbotham paid the score and they set off, he holding her rather tightly by the elbow, since she seemed to find it difficult to negotiate the crossings. As did he.

At the far end of the boulevard, where the smart shops and cafes gave way to less salubrious establishments, such as a bijou cinema advertising Miss Greta Garbo in a movie entitled *Flesh and the Devil*, a music hall promising the delights of *chanteuses, siffleuses, conjuratrices, danseuses nues* and *feu d'artifice*, they came upon a Wax Museum, in whose window there was placed a figure in an armchair (representing God knows whom) that so resembled Uncle Luigi as to bring them both to a halt and the exchange of serious and tipsy speculations, contingent upon which they repaired into the museum and, bearding the proprietor, curator or whatever—a hunchbacked dwarf with a merry eye and a keen sense of humour, who instantly discerned their inebriated condition—were permitted to go into the display window and assure themselves, by pinching and prodding, that the figure was made of wax, indeed, and was not the missing uncle. The dwarf watched them go with a shake of the head and a puckish grin.

By devious tracks, stopping at every gentleman's outfitter's window to scan the dummy figures postured therein, they came at length to the Hôtel de Paris. Back home.

"I think, Annabel," declared Rowbotham, "that the time has come when we must apprise the constabulary of the missing *corpus delicti.*"

"Mmmm?" Her lovely, myopic eyes met his eyes, waveringly.

"Inform the coppers that we've lost Uncle," he said. "I'll telephone them from my suite."

They went up together, to his suite, Annabel still hanging on to his arm. With some difficulty, he was able to put the key into the lock and open up the door.

Beyond the ornate door, a vestibule done out with a lot of Louis Seize furniture, Persian rugs, Gobelins tapestries, gilt sconces, etcetera. Beyond that, the drawing-room.

In the middle of the drawing-room, centered on a tiger-skin rug, stood a wheelchair—*the* wheelchair—with Uncle Luigi seated there as ever. And it seemed to Ernest Rowbotham that the blank eyes held a touch of disfavour.

CHAPTER 8

When he woke, the thin sun of dawn was creeping in through the slats of the venetian blinds. He tried to raise his head from the pillow, but was immediately assailed by a steam-hammer pounding inside his brain. He lay back again with a groan. The sound, the movement caused something—someone—to stir at his elbow. He turned his head and saw to his alarm that he was not alone in the splendid, silk-draped tester bed with its high baldachin surmounted by plaster cherubs and a faun. She was lying with her back to him, her dark hair spread out over the pillow. She was—as far as he could see, and he could see a fair way—nude; the deep declivity of her shapely back continued in sight to the slender waist and beyond. Searching himself, he found that he was in the same state.

Alarmed to move lest he would awaken her, he craned his neck only a little in order to check on the clothing that lay strewn between the open door of the bedroom and the place where they lay.

There was his silk suit, shirt, tie, underpants, socks. And mingled in with them were *her* garments: the striped frock that she had worn during their adventures the previous afternoon, together with sundry items of lightweight female attire that Rowbotham knew only through the medium of illustrated literature confiscated from licentious schoolboys.

Their adventures of the previous afternoon! The phrase

brought the memories crowding back to his much-abused brain.

Surely—he had lost Uncle Luigi!

But then—surely, also, they had found him again? . . .

Focussing with some difficulty, he addressed his vision towards the open door and beyond. Beyond, in the drawing-room, in the middle of the tiger-skin rug, sat Uncle Luigi in his wheelchair—mercifully, with his back to the scene within the bedroom.

"Oh, thank God!" exclaimed Rowbotham aloud.

This brought his bedmate awake; she sat up, hugging the sheets to her bosom, blue-violet eyes wide with a sudden realisation. Then she sank back against the pillow and laughed.

"What's so funny?" asked Rowbotham.

"It's the idea," she said presently, "of the two of us ending up here in bed together. And do you know what? . . ."

"No—what?"

"I think we maybe both fell asleep the moment our heads touched the pillows."

Rowbotham searched his mind—and found nothing. "I think you're probably right," he said. "At least, I've no recollection of us . . ."

"Neither have I!

"What time is it?" she asked presently.

He looked at his wrist-watch. "Half past five."

"I'm rather cold," she said. "Do you mind reaching for the eiderdown and covering us over?"

He did so.

"I'm still not very warm," she said.

"Perhaps if I came a little closer," he said. And did.

"Mmmm. That's better," she said.

After a while—and he was gazing up at the baldachin and speculating upon many things, things like: how can a man go so long through life without putting to the test the way he felt at this living moment, the warmth, the sense of softness, the sudden joy?—she shrank away from him slightly.

"I expect you're much looking forward to seeing that woman again next week," she said.

"Oh, you mean Désirée."

"Charming name."

"Well, actually, her real name's Doris."

"A nice name, but doesn't have quite the exotic ring as Désirée."

"No."

"Did you find her—ah—agreeable?" she asked. And he was aware that she had shrunk away from him even further, and the whole wild waste of the Atlantic Ocean might have lain between them, and, tyro though he was, Rowbotham knew that the outcome of their present circumstance depended upon his next answer.

"Um—she's not very well versed in rolling stock," he said.

"In *rolling* stock?"

"And one could fault her—one could fault her very gravely —for her appreciation of tank engines. The once popular Precursor tank engine and four-six-two and two-four-two engines, their tremendous possibilities, seem to be a closed book to her. She is interested, only, in express locomotives. Albeit, she dabbles in the exotica, such as the vintage Singlewheelers. But that is an elegance, merely. We spent a happy couple of hours."

She sat up in bed, heedless of her nudity, and looked down at him with her misty, blue-violet eyes.

"Are you telling me, Ernest Rowbotham," she said, "that you spent a large part of the afternoon with that high-priced *fille de joie* doing nothing but discussing railway trains?"

"She's very sound on the Great Western," said Rowbotham.

"I'm so happy for her," responded Annabel, and relaxed against him, her shapely arms enfolding his waist, fingers tenderly scrabbling. "Trains are such fun."

From around five-thirty onwards, the starlings had been whistling and chortling in the pine trees behind the hotel. One of them had a particularly irritating refrain: "Charchie-charchie," he went. "Charchie-charchie"—over and over and over again.

A floor above the suite where Ernest Rowbotham and Annabel Smith were being mutually initiated into arcane rites that were entirely their own business, Liza Carlos was woken by the sound and irritably nudged her bedmate.

"Go fix me a cup of coffee, Larry," she ordered. "And while you're about it, I'll have a shot of bourbon on the side. After that, I would like ham and two eggs—sunny side up, as usual. Why do you tarry?"

"All right, all right." Larry Rattazini levered himself stiffly out of the bed and padded over to the kitchenette, pausing only at the bathroom on the way.

"You've been thinking all night," he said. "I can always tell when you're thinking at night, on account of you twist and turn around a lot." Her answer, if answer there was, was lost by the noise of the lavatory flushing.

He made coffee for them both in the neatly fitted-out kitchenette, poured out two hefty jiggers of bourbon, switched on the grill to await the receipt of ham and eggs in the proximate future and returned to the bedroom with coffee and bourbon on a tray.

"I am concerned," she said, "that Nicky Pavese and his hoods are already here before us. It was smart of Aldo to spot them in the bar last night, for it gives us the advantage of surprise. Not too much cream and plenty of sugar."

"What do we do about that mob?" asked Larry.

She stared at him in some surprise, her perfect, though greatly amended, countenance expressing that—nothing more, neither hate nor malevolence, nor, on the other hand, either mercy or compassion.

"We rub them out!" she said.

"*Here?*" he asked.

"Here—today," she replied, laying aside her coffee-cup and downing the shot glass of bourbon in one swallow. "Set it up with the boys. I haven't come all this way to have a louse like Nicky Pavese snatch Luigi's loot right from under my nose."

"Jeeze, but you want that loot, don't you?" he said. "For that, you come all this way. It has to be more than revenge for Luigi killing Francesco—am I right?" He was looking at her cunningly, meaningly, sidelong.

She lit a cigarette and matched his gaze. "You have been snooping around like some kind of louse, you louse," she said.

"I've overheard a thing or two on the grapevine," he admitted. "You know how it is in Chicago—a dame can't change her pants without there's some speculation as to where she left behind the other pair."

Liza blew out a mouthful of smoke and watched it rise in two perfect rings to the elegantly moulded plasterwork of the ceiling.

"I cheated on Francesco but the once," she said, "and that was with Luigi Gaudi. It was all over in a week, and then the rat left me high and dry without so much as a phone call or a postcard. Francesco was in Detroit at the time and never got wind of the affair. Less than a week later, Luigi had him gunned down. He sent me Francesco's ears and the dirty poem.

"The dirty poem concerned me and him!" she shouted.

A long silence followed between them.

"Okay," said Larry at length. "We rub out Nicky Pavese

and his mob today. Tomorrow, or earlier, we lean on the Limey and get him to sing."

"And then I'm going to take a close look at that thing in the wheelchair," said Liza, "which I am convinced is going to turn out to be a dummy."

"And then we look around for the real Luigi—which shouldn't be too difficult. Even in Monte Carlo, which seems to specialise in geriatrics, there can't be all that many guys in wheelchairs." Her dark eyes blazed. "And I would know Luigi Gaudi anywhere. *Anywhere!*"

More pillow talk that same morning in the Hôtel de Paris . . .

Nicky Pavese and his boys shared two double-bedded rooms, not from any exotic proclivity on their parts, but simply to keep down the cost of their mission, which they were having to run on a shoe-string—for reasons that emerged when Nicky jabbed his bedmate in the back to summon him to wakefulness and an harangue:

"Wake up, you bum!" he growled. "Whyfor should *you* sleep while I'm here staring up at the ceiling with my guts churning around and my mind adding and subtracting columns of figures like I was some two-bit clerk? Like I've been doing all night, with you snoring there after the manner of a hog."

"What's the trouble, Nicky?" asked the other—it was the tall, thin and wall-eyed Abie.

"The trouble, brainstorm, is that unless we crack this thing before the end of the week, I'm going to have to put my diamond ring in hock to settle the hotel bill, failing which we are going to have to do a moonlight flit to some cheaper joint. Which will be a pity, because we will no longer be able to keep a close eye on our quarry."

"So?"

"So, genius, we are going to have to crack this thing. One attempt we have made to lean on the Limey, and if you guys had not been so intent upon watching the grass grow, the butterflies mate and other natural phenomena, you might have caught him when he panicked and ran. What happens now is that we're going to have to grab him again—and that ain't going to be so easy second time round, not now that he's wise to our kindly intentions upon his person and his bankroll. COME IN!" he shouted, as there came a discreet tap upon the door.

The man Boris entered, he of the ill-fitting false teeth. Excitement—or the teeth—made his articulation difficult:

"Nicky," he began, "I thought you should know—"

"I told you to keep watch on the Limey's door from daylight onwards and follow him wherever he goes and phone me back!" blazed Nicky. "You are not telling me that you have entrusted this task to Elephant, who will undoubtedly not only lose the quarry but get himself accidentally signed up in the French Foreign Legion for twelve years?"

Boris shook his head. "No, Nicky, Elephant is fast asleep right now. What I came to tell you is that a frail just came out of the Limey's room and went back upstairs. I checked on her going into her room."

"Well, what do you know?" was Nicky's comment. "I had that guy figured for a fairy. Are we cognizant with this broad, Boris?"

Boris's narrow brow was instantly puckered with puzzlement as he contemplated the question. "Well," he said, "I had it in my mind that this was the frail who flashed past us in the sports car when we was chasing the Limey, and picked him up. Same clothes, you know what I mean? But just now, she'd kind of mussed up her hair and taken off her glasses. She don't look like a dog any more. Quite the dish."

Nicky Pavese climbed out of bed in his black silk monogrammed pyjamas and strode across the room to the window, where he stood for a while, hands clasped behind his back, head thrust forward, contemplating the scene outside after the manner of Napoleon taking his last look at Europe from the deck of H.M.S. *Bellerophon*.

Presently he turned, and drove a fist into the palm of the other hand. The bright, clever eyes were sparking fireworks.

"I got it!" he said. And then, with slightly less conviction: "At least, I think I *might* have got it."

Ernest Rowbotham, shaved, bathed, scented with the rarest cologne that the Hôtel de Paris could provide, strode up and down the room with a towel wrapped around his middle. Uncle Luigi, still seated in his wheelchair in the middle of the tiger-skin rug, was the mute recipient of the other's allocution, which was diverse as to subject matter and began with a question:

"How the dickens did you find your way back here, Uncle? I mean, who in all Monte Carlo would take the trouble to bring you home from out of the street, or even *know* that you were staying here at the Paris?

"Now"—shaking a forefinger at the still figure—"don't you try and tell me that one of the hotel staff off duty happened across you in the boulevard, and, having seen you around this place, brought you back to our suite. I thought of that one, and just now I rang the duty manager and put the question to him more or less directly. If one of the staff had brought you back, he would have known about it, but he didn't.

"So who *did* bring you back, Uncle Luigi?"

The figure in the wheelchair predictably keeping its own counsel, Rowbotham strode up and down a couple more times, then wheeled around and pointed again at it.

"And while we're about it, may I say that you did a fine job by setting me and the Universal Dogs' Home of Cincinnati at each other's throats! And the drafting of that will—ye gods! If I want to keep your legacy, I have to spend the rest of my life traipsing from the Casino to *thés dansants,* from *thés dansants* to whore's boudoirs and on and on." He flourished a slip of paper that he had lately removed from the sealed envelope of the day. "I see that tonight you want me to take you to—I quote—'The ritziest night-club in Monte Carlo, with the special proviso that it has to be one where the showgirls appear without their brassières.'

"You dirty-minded old cadaver, Uncle Luigi! My mother and Aunt Angelina would be *ashamed* of you!

"And that isn't the worst of it." He strode up and down a few more times. "Now I've become involved with Annabel. We've been to bed together, and I suppose we shall go to bed together again tonight. It's all your fault! It's all your fault!

"Do you know what? I think I'm stuck on her. And what's more, I've half a notion that she's rather keen on me. But what kind of life is it, I ask you, Uncle Luigi, to offer a girl?—stuck here in Monte Carlo and going the rounds with you, night after bloody night, week after bloody week, in and out of night-clubs, whores' bedrooms and the damned Casino!"

He made a despairing gesture and went to get dressed.

They were sprinkling the emerald green lawns at the Monte Carlo Sporting Club. Down on the foreshore, young boys of the kind whom Rowbotham and Annabel had commissioned to find the missing Uncle Luigi were scouring the beach for valuables that might have been dropped there. They also searched the lapping shallows, where sometimes they found interesting bits of driftwood that they were able to sell to visitors; sometimes they found bodies washed ashore.

In the superb restaurant of the Paris, breakfast was being served to those who preferred to be seen, rather than loll around in bed with a tray. There, in Palm Beach suits and morning frocks, they faced the wearisome choice of London haddie in cream, butterfish meunière, halibut portugaise, devilled kidneys, kedgeree, shirred eggs princesse, pan-fried hash cakes, fourteen types of bread and—the final touch—anything, but anything in the world they fancied.

At nine o'clock, the sound of a bugle from on high announced that they were Changing the Guard up there outside the Palace of the Principality.

At their table in the corner, under a chandelier whose thousand crystal droplets tinkled distantly to the mere tread of the soft-footed waiters, sat Rowbotham and Uncle Luigi in his wheelchair. On this occasion, Annabel had joined them for breakfast and was taking only coffee and a croissant. To Rowbotham's eyes, she looked adorable, for she had left her hair unbound save only by a silk bandeau; she had taken off her glasses and was wearing a dress of beige linen that subtly announced the nuances of her voluptuous form.

Seized by a most extravagant desire, he reached out his hand towards her across the sheer white napery. Annabel's hand met his half-way and squeezed it tenderly.

Uncle Luigi stared sightlessly before him, oblivious to the shirred eggs princesse and pan-fried hash cakes that were going cold on his plate.

CHAPTER 9

The Great War of 1914-18 had greatly changed the fortunes of Monte Carlo. The collapse of the Russian Empire, which reduced those princes and grand dukes who survived the revolution to the roles of emigrant doormen, chauffeurs, *maîtres d'* and the like (and the pre-war Russian aristocracy had been among the biggest gamblers in Europe), together with the dismemberment of the German and Austro-Hungarian domains, rid the Principality of its most abundant sources of income. What largely remained of it came from the ever-present English, plus the new influx of dollar millionaires. But even these gentry found themselves inclined more towards the cheaper and less formal delights of Juan-les-Pins, Nice, Antibes. Add to that the annual migration of high-priced cocottes, the *grandes horizontales* from Paris, who had so delighted the Edwardian gentry of pre-war days, found themselves outdistanced by the post-war freedom of choice won by women of all classes. What man will look to a whore when even duchesses and members of the Social Register are up to it for free? There remained such as little Doris alias Désirée, but they were in the minority compared with the rich and titled amateurs waiting down the road in Nice.

It was to stem this slide from former greatness that the newly appointed administrator M. René Léon set in train a programme to recapture the pre-eminence that the Principality had formerly enjoyed in the Riviera. He appointed a new president of the Sporting Club, encouraged the building of a new casino with a sliding roof open to the sky, which was opened by King Gustav of Sweden and adorned on that same occasion by the singing of the American diva Miss Grace Moore. He opened the Country Club, which set Monte Carlo as the Mecca of sport in the Riviera. Imported chorines, the Monte Carlo Rally and Grand Prix added to the Principality's lustre. The great boom days returned again.

One of M. Léon's innovations was the sumptuous night-club called the Schéhérazade, and it was to the Schéhérazade that, following upon instructions, Ernest Rowbotham took his Uncle Luigi that evening, and Annabel Smith accompanied them.

"I don't know what men make all the fuss about," murmured Annabel with a touch of petulance. "When you've seen one pair of woman's bosoms, you've seen them all. I think I shall go and powder my nose."

She went, leaving Rowbotham to contemplate upon her observation in the light of the evidence posturing and prancing, bobbing and jouncing, on the dance floor a few yards from where he sat: eight girls clad in the most elaborate costumes and head-dresses; head-dresses that towered to the ceiling in elaborations of flora and fauna, costumes that trailed trains of flounce and fancy—but all of them deficient in the area of the thorax, which was left uncovered in every case.

Eight pairs. He mulled the evidence over, and came to the conclusion—a great truth that every man arrives at sooner or later, depending upon the range of his experience: "There aren't two pairs of them alike!" he murmured aloud. "Have you noticed that, Uncle Luigi?"

Further scientific enquiry being cut short by the departure of the showgirls and the return of Annabel, Rowbotham addressed himself, after a little small talk with her, to their surroundings, the lights now having been raised so that it was almost possible to discern the limits of the smoke-filled room through the Stygian gloom. At the far end from them, beyond the dance floor, which was being filled by circling couples foxtrotting to the strains of "Yes, Sir, That's My Baby" rendered by an ensemble that announced itself as Les Garçons du Jazz, stood the buffet table, presided over by a quartette of servitors in chef's costume. There was a confection of seafood: lobster piled upon lobster, prawns spilling like manna from heaven in between, all set upon a bed of oysters, clams and scallops and garnished with—only the French could think of it—a profusion of pink roses.

"Mr. Rowbotham, how's it going?" Rowbotham looked round to see his friend of the Casino standing at his elbow, and got up to shake his hand.

"Just fine, Mr. Bragg. And you?"

Introductions followed, and Ezekiel Bragg consented to sit with them and have a drink, though, as he was quick to point out: "I'm hell-bent for the Casino, where I've been on that winning streak ever since I met you there. How about that, Miss Smith? Ernest here has really brought me luck, and I'm going to ride along with it till I come to the end of the lode. I'm not even staying to hear Maurice Chevalier."

Annabel smiled indulgently upon them both. She really does look simply super-duper tonight, thought Rowbotham. The way she's got her hair, that black frock. Those eyes! She makes every other woman in the room appear like someone up from the country selling eggs. Not that one can really see anyone properly in this gloom. Though I have to admit that that somewhat mature brunette over there, the one in a golden frock, is pretty striking. Mmmm, she's noticed me staring in her direction. Better shift my gaze before her escort comes over and dots me on the nose . . .

Three tables away, Liza Carlos sat with Larry Rattazini,

she in a gold lamé sheath-dress that did wonders for her unbelievably slender figure.

"So that's Rowbotham?" she murmured. "And the alleged Luigi, my sometime inamorato, is the thing with its back to us in the wheelchair. Who is the good-looking guy with the moustache talking to the dame?"

"I don't have anything on him," said Rattazini, "but the dame is one Annabel Smith, unmarried, American, staying also at the Paris."

"And the Nicky Pavese mob?"

"Way over there," replied the other. "In the far corner. Four silhouettes as you see them, and they can't see us. This I fixed with the hall porter when they had him ring through and book them in at the Schéhérazade. I slipped him a greenback and he saw to it that they had the worst table in the house. It's also directly in line"—he inclined his head upwards and backwards—"with the balcony."

"Where Aldo and Poeta await?"

"With the Equaliser. One five-second burst should be enough."

"When?"

"In the middle of the star turn of the evening, when the floor's clear and everyone's attention's on the guy in the spotlight."

"And the Pavese mob still don't know we're here?"

"Not so far as I know. It scarcely matters, does it? We have them on toast tonight. With them rubbed out, we then move in on Rowbotham and Luigi."

"If that thing is Luigi," said Liza Carlos, "I am Elsa Maxwell. I still stick to the view that Rowbotham holds the fortune and that the real, live Luigi is waiting around in his Bath chair to collect." She smiled, and it was the smile of Medusa. "I could almost feel it in my heart to be sorry for the guy—to have to spend the rest of his days a cripple in some poor-house. Teach him to send me the dirty poem!"

They dined off green turtle soup followed by vol-au-vent. Uncle Luigi was served with a dozen oysters followed by frogs' legs—by his special request in the note of instruction. They were, of course, sent back uneaten.

"What are we going to do, Annabel?" asked Rowbotham, half-heartedly pushing his dessert, a pecan nut sundae, around his plate.

"Do you mean what are we going to do about Uncle Luigi?" she countered. "Or about *us*?"

He met her steady gaze. "The both issues seem to be inextricably entwined," he said.

"Do you want Uncle Luigi's fortune very badly, Ernest?"

"Do you want the Universal Dogs' Home of Cincinnati to have it very badly, Annabel?" he riposted.

"While I work for them, while I draw a salary, yes I do," she replied. "I wouldn't be true to myself if I did otherwise."

"You could resign."

"And?"

The question hung in the air. It is possible that an angel, passing over, paused in his flight to hear what came next.

"You could marry me," he said.

"And remain in Monte Carlo for the rest of our lives, with another agent from the Dogs' Home monitoring everything you do?" she replied. "With you hopping off to the *thé dansant* every Wednesday afternoon, followed by railway discussions with Miss Désirée? Do you see me in the role of spouse under these conditions? Don't get me wrong, darling, Monte Carlo is a charming, a delightful place. I would be perfectly happy to live here. But not with *him* in the guest bedroom." She indicated Uncle Luigi bowed over his untouched Canton pudding. "Nor with the eternal roundelay that his stupid lawyers have condemned you to."

Rowbotham thought for a while and said: "It's the best option I can offer you, Annabel. The other is that of wife to a not very successful assistant master at the kind of low-grade private school that only England has the genius to produce.

"I speak of getting out of bed on to cold lino in the mornings, of breakfasting off tepid scrambled eggs, burnt toast and bottled coffee essence; of snotty-nosed, leery, spotty boys who will be lurking to watch you undress unless you're careful to draw your curtains; ice-cold chapel on Sundays, and a ranting preacher of a headmaster who's cheating his wife with the housemaid.

"I've been through it all, Annabel. In fact, I've been through it twice, both as boy and master, and rather than go through it again, I would happily starve on a park bench, or traipse Uncle Luigi till the day I die."

"There doesn't seem a lot more to say, does there?" she replied.

He shook his head.

He rose when she rose; made an attempt to drape her silk paisley shawl about her shoulders, but she forestalled him, avoided the touch of his hand, drew aside her cheek when he attempted to plant a kiss there.

"I'll see you out," he said. "And get you a taxi."

"Please don't bother," she said. "I'm quite capable. Stay and look after your corpse."

And she was gone.

There was more ecdysialism: Rowbotham was given plenty of opportunity to ponder, in the exotic *spectacles* that followed, upon his thesis that no two persons of the female persuasion carry under their blouses an identical treasure chest; Uncle Luigi, at some distance, may have confirmed the same conclusion. The lights being further dimmed almost to extinction during these demonstrations, he was no longer able to see the dramatic brunette of mature years, at the table thrice removed, with the gentleman who bore a scar upon his cheek, who had noticed him staring at her earlier.

Glumly, he pondered upon his break with Annabel—for break it surely had been. He had proposed to her—well, more or less proposed to her—and had been soundly rejected on the score of Uncle Luigi.

Was there no other way out? No other options?

"I could ditch you, Uncle," he said aloud to his mutely amiable companion, "but it wouldn't seem really fair. It's very odd and silly, the way I've got quite fond of you, your dirty mind and all.

"I s'pose, I s'pose, in a way, you are playing out all the fantasies that most chaps harbour in their hearts: the craving for fame, for fortune, for the love of fair women. And because of this I can't possibly ditch you, Uncle.

"As for Annabel—well, I still think she's stuck on me, and I know I'm stuck on her, and I'm sure a way can be found. Only . . ."

Chin in hand, he gazed long and hard into the visage of the thing in the chair.

"If only that undertaker chap in Chicago had taken the trouble to pretty you up a bit, we might have made a *ménage à trois*."

The instructions stipulated that they stay till the end of the cabaret, followed by the English conceit of a fried-bacon-and-eggs breakfast, which was served around four in the morning. Rowbotham resigned himself to the chore. The fair ecdysiasts, in any event, were no hardship; less tolerable were a troupe of Chinese acrobats, a man who played a nose-flute, and a gentleman who, having placed a handsome Negress in a chest, proceeded to saw her in half, chest and all.

Finally, with a fair amount of fanfaronade, the star of the evening stepped on to the scene; dazzling in a well-cut tuxedo, jaunty straw boater, lower lip jutting piquantly.

> *"Eeef the Sand-man brought me dreams of you,*
> *Ah'd want to sleep mah whole life through . . ."*

Up on the balcony that circled half of that plush-lined cellar, Poeta Minghetti nodded to his companion Aldo Ricasoli, and the latter cocked the action of the Thompson sub-machine-gun that he carried with him. There was no one else on the balcony, which was only used as an overspill on high days and holidays, like Bastille Day and so forth. No one had seen them go up there, and one straight flight of steps gave them egress to the alley-way behind the club.

"Can you see them plain, Aldo?"

"Like they was in a shooting-gallery," responded the other. "Just four cut-out figures with the light behind 'em. What I'll do is stitch from left to right at chest level. A five-second burst, like Larry told me—that'll fix 'em real fine."

"You okay, Aldo? You been hitting that hip-flask of bourbon ever since we was here. You want that I should take over the job?"

The other shook his head. "Poeta, when I have had a coupla drinks, I am very much more organized, know what I mean? F'rinstance, you will recall that Christmas Day job on Laramie and Lawrence, when we busted in on the Touhy mob, not because there was a nickel in it for anybody, but just part of the Christmas spirit."

"Aldo, I remember it well," responded his companion. "We bust into that hotel. Outnumbered four to one. Blasted that dinner party. Rubbed out Giolitti and Luzzatti—"

"Luzzatti, he was playing Santa Claus, handing out presents to the kids from the Christmas tree."

"It was a lovely way to go. I couldn't ask for better."

"And then we made our get-away."

"And you were driving the automobile. Man, how you drove that car! With all the Touhy fleet right behind you, you led them a dance from Lawrence to Cicero and nearly the goddamned way to Burnham. Man, you drove that night!

"I was stoned out of my mind on that occasion."

"You are putting me on."

"Absolutely no, Poeta. I was soaked to the gills. Like I explained you, I am very much more organized when I have imbibed. As you will see . . ."

He steadied his left arm against the balcony, took sight along the stubby barrel of the sub-machine-gun, put first pressure on the trigger.

Mr. Gordon Selfridge and the Dolly sisters were occupying a plushy banquette in a discreet corner. The tycoon had one hand upon the silk-clad knee of Miss Jenny, and the other on that of her sibling at his other side. This meant that he was left with no hand with which to pick up his drink, save to abandon the knee of one or other lady for a short while. He had long ago solved this problem: he abandoned the knee of each alternately. The action was observed by both ladies, and the alternation rigorously counted. There are tremendous pressures upon the very rich.

Rowbotham said: "Uncle, as soon as this French chap's finished warbling, I'm going outside for a breath of fresh air. It may not be worrying you, but the tobacco smoke in this room could be cut up into slices and vended piecemeal."

He had hardly finished when the shooting started . . .

Aldo's theory about his increased efficiency when drunk was, like so many illusions held by hard drinkers, entirely illusory. His first burst, due to the fact that the savage recoil of the weapon took him entirely by surprise, hit the wall ten feet to the left of and five feet above the heads of the Nicky Pavese mob, who, hardened mobsters as they were, well versed in the social niceties of the Windy City, immediately hit the deck.

The Dolly sisters fainted upon the instant.

Rowbotham, who was more or less in the line of fire (he heard the .45-calibre slugs zap past his ear), similarly adopted a recumbent posture, but in doing so collided with Uncle Luigi's wheelchair. The chair had a brake, but Rowbotham had not given any thought to applying it, for where and when is there any traffic hazard in a night-club?

The wheelchair, free of any encumbrance, rolled slowly backwards, and Uncle Luigi perforce went with it. Up on the balcony, Aldo Ricasoli, having snapped another magazine into his Thompson, essayed another burst in the—to him—general direction of the Pavese mob, who had by this time cleared well out of the way on their bellies.

The first slugs demolished the most intricate and elegant confection of seafood at the buffet table, creating a downfall of lobsters, prawns, clams, scallops, pink roses, as would have fed an indigent family of six for a month. The second burst reduced to ruin an enormous creation of pêche Melba, which collapsed under the assault like an Alpine avalanche, most of it landing in the lap of the clarinettist of Les Garçons du Jazz, who was in the proximate vicinity.

The third burst hit Uncle Luigi fair and square as he was borne slowly backwards across the dance floor.

The Dolly sisters, having achieved no very great attention by their fainting act, began to scream. A lot of ladies were screaming.

Maurice Chevalier, seemingly unperturbed, carried on with his act:

"*Everee leetle breeze seems to whispair Louise,
Birds in the trees seem to whispair Louise . . .*"

Commissaire Paul Darré, having heard from his wife's very expensive obstetrician that—contingent upon a familial tendency on both their sides, together with certain early signs—it was highly likely she would be blessed with twins, had withdrawn every sou that could be spared from his bank account and had essayed it all, that afternoon, in the Casino, playing a system which is known as *Tiers et tout à la boule de neige*, an interesting method of play which consists of dividing one's stake—in Darré's case two thousand francs—into two parts of one and two thirds respectively. Playing *chances simples*, one then doubles up on one's bet if one loses at the first *coup*, and reverts to the original stake on the second, win or lose. It has the advantage, over such methods as the Martingale, the Labouchère and the Paroli, that one wins or loses quite slowly. Darré lost his two thousand in about three hours.

He was slumped in his office chair, contemplating the service revolver in his locked drawer, the same that he had carried as an officer of the 2e Chasseurs in the hell of Verdun, when Martin burst in. The excitement, the urgency, on the other's countenance and the manner of his address precluded all reproof.

"Chief, there's been a shooting at the Schéhérazade!"

"It had to happen sooner or later. I should apply for them to close that joint."

Martin looked sly, the way he often did when he was about to deliver a bombshell. "It was carried out with a sub-machine-gun," he said. "The same as the one that was used in the Orange-road murders."

"Don't tell me this!"

"True, Chief! Our fellows found a hundred spent forty-five-calibre cartridge cases up in the balcony. That's two whole drums of Thompson ammunition."

"How many killed?"

Martin looked disappointed. "No one, Chief."

"Who, then, was the target for this fusillade? Where was it directed?"

"Difficult to say, Chief. The gunman was pretty liberal with his aim. But one thing's for sure . . ."

"And what is that?"

"The Mrs. Liza Carlos and Mr. Lawrence J. Rattazini of whom I have spoken to you before were not directly involved in the shooting, either as participants or recipients. They were dining together and not in the line of general fire. And the fire was pretty general, I tell you. Some of the bullets must have only narrowly missed Maurice Chevalier, who was singing at the time, and kept on singing through it all."

"Well, the gunman surely wasn't aiming at Chevalier," said Darré. "He's not *that* bad."

CHAPTER 10

"Well, if you hadn't snuffed it already, Uncle Luigi, tonight would have done for you for sure!"

They were back in their suite at the Paris, Charles the chauffeur having picked them up from the Schéhérazade at the appointed time of 5 A.M. Strictly according to instructions, Rowbotham had ingested eggs and bacon *à l'anglaise* while his uncle had contemplated the same. The police had come. There had been questioning, and Rowbotham had been questioned. Fortunately, they had not questioned Uncle Luigi, and had accepted his nephew's assertion that the poor old fellow had fallen asleep immediately the uncamisoled showgirls had finished their act and before Chevalier had commenced his. They had not noticed that the "sleeper's" tailcoat and vest were riddled with bullet holes because Rowbotham had had the prescience to cover the damage with a napkin. There was, of course, no blood. Apart from riddling a mummified cadaver, bringing down a tremendous amount of wall plaster and decimating a mountain of crustaceans and dessert, it could be said that the shooting had been a sheer waste of time and bullets. The assailants got clean away.

"I'm going to ring Annabel," declared Rowbotham upon an impulse. "And I simply can't wait till a civilised hour."

He connected with her room. The phone rang out for scarcely more than a few seconds.

"Annabel, this is Ernest. I'm sorry to wake you up."

"I wasn't asleep. I haven't been asleep all night. I've been ringing you every half hour."

"Oh—Annabel!" The grey dawn cleared, and the sunlight washed over him. How could he have wasted so much of his life in shadows? he asked himself.

"Every half hour," she said. "I couldn't wait to tell you that I was wrong. That I'd live in Monte Carlo all my life—Uncle Luigi, Désirée and her trains, the Schéhérazade, Casino and all—rather than go back to Cincinnati and no you."

"I'll come up to you now," he said. "Is that all right?"

"Yes, now. Quickly."

He replaced the receiver. "Well, Uncle Luigi, I'm going to leave you now," he said. "I don't expect you'll come to much harm, but we're going to have to address ourselves to changing your bullet-riddled clothes and that might be rather unpleasant. However, for the time being, you'll have to put up with things the way they are.

"I don't know whether you are aware, on whatever celestial plane you are sitting, that everything's all right between Annabel Smith and me again, and that we shall almost certainly get married. You will be part of the ménage, though (and I hope you won't take this ill, for, as you know, I've grown tremendously fond of you in an odd sort of way) I would wish it otherwise.

"I wonder—I wonder if it might be possible to set you up in another establishment? That's not a bad notion. One could employ someone—Charles, for instance—to live with you and look after you, while I continue with the requirements of the will, which, after all, don't *really* impose a restriction on one's life-style much beyond being an active member of, for instance, a golf-club, or a particularly active madrigal society. Yes, that's worth thinking about. I'll put it to Annabel, and find out from her if the idea in any way contravenes the terms of the will.

"Good morning to you, Uncle. See you later."

On the way out of the door, he stumbled and almost fell over a sizeable hard object lying there. Stooping to pick it up, he found it to be a rock, or stone, irregularly shaped, about the size of, say, a hen's egg. It was dullish yellow-white in colour, and not of pleasing appearance. He dropped it into a waste-paper basket and gave it no more thought, but went on his way to his tryst with Annabel Smith, who awaited his coming in a black lace confection that she had hastily put on at the close of their phone conversation.

"Liza Carlos, it was, who set us up," declared Nicky Pavese. He slapped his forehead with the palm of his hand and pulled an expression of saintly anguish. "Why didn't I figure it that Liza would muscle in on this deal, particularly since her old man was rubbed out by Luigi Gaudi? They were in the night-club. You guys saw them—Liza and that rat Rattazini—when the lights went up after the shooting had finished. They've been playing cat and mouse with us all this time, here at this hotel, keeping out of our sight, waiting for the chance to rub us all out and score a home run to Luigi's dough. I'm here to tell you, friends all, that but for the intervention of kindly fate—such as the guy who fired that Equaliser was either boozed out of his small mind, or else he should be wearing pebble glasses of the thickest sort—we would at this time be lying on four cold slabs at the local morgue, awaiting the kindly ministrations of the post-mortem cowboy's scalpel, I kid you not."

"We'll blast Liza and her bums!" growled wall-eyed Abie, taking a deep swig of his breakfast gin.

"Yah—dat's right!" seconded Elephant, nodding.

"What about it, Nicky?" asked Boris, who deferred to his ringleader in everything and seldom put up a proposition. "Do we burst into their suite and blast 'em?"

"Too crude," replied Nicky Pavese. "What, my friends, is the object of this mission of ours? The question is not merely rhetorical, but open to free comment. You do not answer? I will enlighten you: the object of this mission is to lay our hands upon Luigi's loot, which, we are convinced, does not lie in a bank but is stashed in notes or in portable valuables in the care of Mr. Limey Rowbotham. That is it, gentlemen. That is all. We are not in business to rub out Liza Carlos and her gorillas—that were only to draw the attention of the local constabulary to our presence. Let Liza Carlos, in the typical manner of the hysterical frail, blow off in all directions. We'll keep ducking. She'll get caught."

"Gee, you make it very clear, Nicky," said Elephant. "I sure wish dat I had your brains and your education."

Disregarding the flattery, Pavese continued his peroration: "Which brings us to my big idea. Now—you will recall that the summons of Mother Nature directed my footsteps to the little boys' room at one stage of last night's proceedings. Upon my return, I chanced upon the Junoesque brunette whom Mr. Limey Rowbotham is currently squiring. This frail was flinging herself out of the club with some velocity, pausing only to snatch up her feather boa from the hat-check girl and dive out to yell for a cab to convey her back to the hotel. And what was more, she was in tears, with the mascara staining her cheeks in black rivulets. What do you make of that?"

Abie poured himself another breakfast gin. "She had just had a fight with the Limey," he submitted.

"That's right," confirmed Boris. "He maybe refused to make an honest woman of her."

"Maybe dey didn't fight over anything very much," proffered Elephant. "Maybe dey just had dis liddle spat, and she was crying on account of she's crazy about him, and maybe he's crazy about her."

Nicky Pavese's clever, bright eyes flared. He pointed

straight at the giant. "Out of the mouths of babes and sucklings comes forth wisdom," he misquoted. "And likewise out of the mouth of this lower anthropoid here present. That's it. That's the sign I have been waiting for. Mr. Limey Rowbotham and the frail known as Miss Annabel Smith are not only romping in bed together, they are also in amorous conjunction.

"And that, my friends, delivers him up into our power—hook, line and sinker!"

They had a private, informal luncheon together on the shady balcony outside the suite: Rowbotham, Annabel and Uncle Luigi. They had a coarse-cut terrine, followed by a simple sole bonne femme, which was good with a Chablis dry as paper. A yard or so out in the sunlight, no more, the cicadas shrilled upon the branches of the pine trees, and far out to sea four J-class yachts dipped their expensive masts in the freshening breeze and scored fingertips of white water in the shimmering blueness, one against the other.

With the coffee and *fine*, Rowbotham opened the envelope for the day which dictated his activities for the evening; Annabel, who possessed a duplicate set, opened hers also.

To his surprise, Rowbotham found, within the envelope, not a half sheet of paper with terse instructions, but a veritable document, and written in the genuine execrable hand:

Chicago, Illinois.
November 18

Dear Nephew Ernest,
You are going to think me crazy. I will explain. When I was a kid on the East Side, and my old man had died of working with yellow asbestos, my mother kept us both by scrubbing floors at Bloomingfeld's store in West 57th, rising at four and working thru till nine when the store

opened, then back again at six thru midnight to serve behind a bar. What a life!

My mother, in her young days, she had been what you would call a hoofer, that's to say a dancer in a travelling troup of vaudeville players. Dancing was her whole life, but she never made out of the chorus line of account that she put on a lot of weight early, also that she was a good Catholic girl and would not help along her career on her back.

When I was six, she sent me to Miss Meinecke's Dance Academy on West 55th. That's Saturday mornings, ten thru twelve at the Teamsters' Union hall, one dollar fifty a lesson on account that Miss Meinecke had used to dance in the Ballet. For this my mother scrubs floors.

Picture the alibis I give to the neighbourhood gang! Fortunately West 55th is a piece away from where we are living, and I tell the guys in the gang that I am taking boxing lessons every Saturday morning. Rather than be branded a sissy, I would have told them that I was out raping nuns.

All would have been fine, but Miss Meinecke decides that the Dance Academy will give a show. And where else but O'Donnel's Egyptian Theater on the corner of our block! Need I say more? You picture me dancing The Sugar Plum Fairy with the gang up there in the gallery? Not me! I walked right out of Miss Meinecke's Dance Academy and kept walking. And it broke my mother's heart, she who had scrubbed floors to see me dance with the Russian Ballet in Monte Carlo along with Nijinsky. She died of that broken heart, of this I am convinced.

Nephew Ernest, it is fixed that I shall appear on stage at the Monte Carlo Opera in a presentation of *The*

Sleeping Beauty, which is a production that admits of plenty walking-on roles. All you have to do on the day you read this is to deliver me to the stage door at seven in time for me to be costumed and made up. And ask for Jean-Pierre. He has been fixed.

Hope you enjoy my performance. You will be watching it from the Royal Box. Mama and me will be watching it from a somewhat higher plane.

Yours ever,
 Uncle Luigi

When Rowbotham had finished reading, he looked up and saw, not entirely to his surprise, that Annabel was in tears.

She laid down her copy of the letter. "I think that's the most touching thing I've ever read," she said. "I really do. Your Uncle Luigi must have been, deep down, a very loving, giving man."

Rowbotham regarded the figure sitting between them: the head bowed, blindly regarding the untouched compote of apricots and the delicate cup of steaming coffee with a little cream added, but no sugar.

"He grows on you," said Rowbotham. "The way he planned this whole thing through, you have to admire him, his single-mindedness, his dedication. And the tone of this letter to me—full of affection, as if we had known each other all my life. I really am quite fond of the old boy, and I'm sure I shall never be able willingly to part with him."

"You won't need to, Ernest," she replied, reaching out her hand and laying it upon his. "We'll keep him with us. Uncle Luigi's no trouble, nor ever will be."

It was a statement which, though sincerely intended, was destined to be wildly wide of the mark.

It was at seven-fifteen of the clock that Aldo Ricasoli rang through to his lady boss in her suite. Liza Carlos was enjoying a post-coital bubble bath, while her first lieutenant and bedmate was fixing a manhattan and a side-car for her and himself respectively. He took the call.

"It's Aldo, babe," he called out. "Says it's important. He tailed the Limey and etcetera out of the hotel just now."

She came out of the bathroom, steaming slightly, bubbles running over and down her smooth, olive skin. "Gimme that drink," she said, "and stop leering at me like I was some cheap shimmy dancer." Into the phone: "Is that you, Aldo. What gives?"

Aldo replied: "We followed them to, would you believe, the Opera House, where there is playing tonight a show called *The Sleeping Beauty*, which, from the pix outside, looks like some kinda musical with hoofers held up by fairies. But this is the puzzling part. Not to the front of the house did they go, but to the stage-door entrance, and there the Limey left Luigi in the care of the stage-door-keeper, by name, as we discovered, Jean-Pierre. Whereupon he then departed with his broad, that's the Smith dame."

"And where did *they* go?"

"They picked up tickets from the front of the house and are now ensconced in the theatre bar, the show not being due to commence till half of eight."

"Get after Luigi!" snapped Liza. "This is the night. This is the night of the pick-up. Either the loot is stashed somewhere in the Opera House—or else . . ."

"Or else what, Liza?" Both men—the man at the other end of the line and the naked man by her side—echoed each other's question.

"Or else the set-up is for Rowbotham to meet *him*—the *real*, live Luigi in his wheelchair—hand over the diamonds, pick up his own cut and depart with the Smith broad."

"You think so, Liza?"

"I almost *know* so," she responded to whichever had posed the question. "Listen here, Aldo. Leave the Limey to Larry and me. Get in that stage door. Get close to that thing in the wheelchair and don't let it out of your sight all night. Okay?"

"Liza, I—"

"What?" Sharply.

"I have to tell you that, though this Jean-Pierre is a little guy, kind of old and weighing around maybe ninety, a hundred pounds, he has an assistant who is built like that torpedo who works for Nicky Pavese, that guy called Elephant, only this one has extra bits stuck on. When Poeta and me tried to get into the stage door, he swept us out like we was garbage."

Liza exhaled loudly through her nostrils. "Listen to me," she said, "and listen good. Get in there. Lean on this extra Elephant guy. That's what Equalisers are all about. Get back there. Get backstage. Find what gives with that thing in the wheelchair. Stay with it. Keep your eyes on it."

"Sure thing, Liza."

"Oh, and by the way . . ."

"Yes, Liza?"

"Speaking of the Pavese mob. Have they shown today?"

"Not as of when we left the hotel on the heels of the Limey and etcetera. They had a Do Not Disturb notice on the door of their suite. I had it from the house dick that they had themselves a party last night and there was complaints from the folks on either side."

"They were probably celebrating their escape from your hot-shot marksmanship," retorted Liza, and, which gibe calling forth no answer, she replaced the phone.

"Larry," she said to her companion. "Tonight, we go to the ballet. Fix us two seats in the orchestra stalls. You in white tie and tails. I shall wear my Paris gown, the Worth backless number. And my rocks."

They were drinking champagne cocktails in the theatre bar; side by side, and he thought she had never looked lovelier—not even on the occasion when she had first opened the door to him with her hair down and minus her glasses.

The "arrangement" had gone surprisingly smoothly: there had indeed been a stage-door-man who answered to the name of Jean-Pierre, who was expecting them, who had obviously been "squared" with bright gold, who made no demur at the prospect of having to costume and make up a corpse that—Rowbotham had felt the delicacy to point out—had recently been riddled with bullets. This had not swerved Jean-Pierre from his intention one whit ("M'sieu, I used to be *un entrepreneur de pompes funèbres,* what you would call a mortician, *hein?*"), and he had departed somewhere into the nether regions of backstage, pushing Uncle Luigi before him, and leaving his stage door to the tender ministrations of the biggest, ugliest and meanest-looking individual—shaven-headed, scowling, truculent—that Rowbotham had ever seen in his life; he felt quite relieved to depart.

In the theatre bar were now gathering the *bon ton* of the resort: several coroneted heads, a prince of a minor royal blood, millionaires undoubted, and all with their wives or doxies. That same British admiral who had witnessed the embarrassing incident in the restaurant car of the Blue Train was with the same handsome widow from Boston, Massachusetts, whom he had met up with on that occasion. The gallant sea-dog had clearly not been wasting the time between, for the widow, Mrs. Willibrand, sported on her engagement finger a splendid emerald and diamond ring; a new ring, which, it has to be said, she had paid for herself, since the admiral was temporarily out of funds till he had sold off a parcel of shares in South African mines—as he had explained.

The Dolly sisters and Mr. Gordon Selfridge were there, at a discreet banquette seat in the corner. Unlike Mrs. Willibrand, the sisters had no new jewellery: their plump little fingers, their shell-like ears, their swan-like necks, had no *room* for any new jewellery!

Serge Diaghilev was there, along with Cocteau and Lifar. The latter was in a silk dressing-gown and already made up for the performance. They drank champagne cocktails and were dismissively amused by everyone they saw around them. Rowbotham's friend of the Casino, the egregious Ezekiel Bragg, was there, and with a very pretty young redhead; he waved to Rowbotham and returned to the discourse with his companion. Five minutes after, the discreet tinkle of a well-tuned carillon announced that the performance was shortly due to begin.

"I hope Uncle Luigi doesn't disgrace himself," said Rowbotham, offering Annabel his arm. "It would be such a pity, after all the trouble he's taken."

The backstage dressing-rooms, varying in size and splendour from those of the principal dancers, through those soloists who merited a certain consideration, to the tightly-packed snuggeries of the *corps de ballet*, were nearly all empty, the performers having drifted stagewards for the tremendous *mise en scène* which provides the opening of *The Sleeping Beauty*. Two only lingered, and these in the middling-rank men's dressing-room. They were costumed and having a quarrel which was rendered in a patois of French and Russian vehemently delivered and, if not actually accompanied with *pliés* and *entrechats dix*, certainly with mimed gestures of tremendous expression that spoke of years and years of slogging hard work and selfless devotion to their demanding art.

They had just about reached the stage of hair-pulling when the door was quickly opened and closed, and two men stood within: one of them tall, thin and wall-eyed; the other short, with badly fitting false teeth that shifted when he enunciated:

"Get back up against the wall, you two fairies—and take off your knickers!" This was Boris, and like Abie he was carrying a pistol.

Five minutes later, as the opening bars of Tchaikovsky's overture were seeping like liquid gold and silver through backstage, Boris and Abie emerged from the dressing-room. Both were now attired in the costumes of courtiers in some never-never land of fairy-tale inhabited by the ballet upon which the curtain was about to rise. It has to be said that the two Chicago gangsters—who were of middle years, and had not been comely even in their salad days—presented an unimposing pair: the purloined tights hung about Abie's skinny shanks like the wrinkled skin of a pug-dog, but fortunately managed to hide his desperate case of varicose veins; while Boris had taken for himself in a hurry the doublet of the taller of the two male dancers, and it fitted him where it touched, which was neither widespread nor frequently.

"There he goes!" hissed Abie, taking his companion by the arm and dragging him behind the concealment of a curtain. "There's the guy Jean-Pierre with Luigi in the wheelchair."

"Luigi has on some kinda fancy costume," said the other.

"So have we, dumb-bell," responded his companion. "It is truly said that the best place to hide a tree is in a forest. Who's gonna question us? We're ballet dancers. Luigi is pulling the same gag, and the guy Jean-Pierre is conniving in the deception. We will keep them both under close observation, as ordered. Let's go."

They followed after the stage-door-keeper and the figure in the wheelchair, which, on closer inspection, they saw to be dressed in the costume of a pierrot, with whitened face, slash of red lips, black skull-cap. As they watched, Jean-Pierre, having brought the wheelchair to the foot of a flight of ornamental steps (and all unobserved by the members of the ballet who were milling about him, absorbed as they were with their appearances, their make-up, their current love affairs, but most of all the dedication to the performances they were about to give), lifted out the slight figure and seated it upon the third step up, propping it against the ornamental balustrade, arranging its legs, laying its arms across its lap. He then made himself swiftly scarce, wheelchair and all.

Boris and Abie, despite their total ignorance of the backstage of a theatre (they thought they were in some kind of annexe to the coming spectacle), became aware of a sudden change in attitude of those around them: a stiffening of posture, an almost imperceptible air of commitment, as when a presumptive knight, having watched over his arms in the night's long vigil, sees the dawn of the day of his accolade; or when a freshly bedded bride, awaiting the return of her groom from the bathroom, hears the flushing of the lavatory and, shrinking, tries to remember the good advice that her mother gave her.

The overture ceased. There was silence. The violins took up the theme of the opening scene. The curtains wafted regally apart.

"Jeeze!" breathed Abie. "We're part of the goddamned show!"

The Royal Box at the Monte Carlo opera enjoys the same benefits and suffers the same shortcomings as Royal Boxes everywhere, that's to say one is revealed to everyone in the house in the setting of a chocolate-box (or a hen-coop), is the cynosure of all eyes and the object of admiration, or envy, or loathing; set against this, the shortcomings are that one truly sees only about two thirds of the spectacle, and in the case of the ballet, the proximity to the performers can sometimes be quite disturbing, for the rigours of the classical dance may be likened to an amalgam of all-in wrestling, weight-lifting and the high jump; at close quarters, the sight of painted faces streaked with sweat does little to aid the willing suspension of disbelief, and the rising odour of perspiring bodies can sometimes be quite overpowering.

Annabel Smith was enchanted. As the curtains swept apart, she clung more tightly to Rowbotham's hand and gasped like a little girl viewing her first pantomime (and, indeed, *The Sleeping Beauty*, as choreographed by Petipa to the score of Tchaikovsky, is really a pantomime for children of all ages), so that he glanced sidelong at her and thought how beautiful she was, how tenderly vulnerable in the way she moistened her lips, and how her eyes shone. And he blessed the Universal Dogs' Home of Cincinnati for sending her to him.

"Look, Ernest—that must be Uncle Luigi," she whispered, and he saw the white-clad, white-faced figure slumped upon the ornamental staircase, as if asleep, or contemplating.

"Well, he won't come to much harm there," responded Rowbotham. "In fact, he looks quite decorative in an odd kind of way."

Across the auditorium, seated in the twin of the Royal Box with his friends, Diaghilev regarded the *mise en scène* through mother-of-pearl opera-glasses and commented to his immediate companion: *"Mon cher* George, you have done a remarkable thing to bring this rather tired old charade alive with your admirable direction. *Quel spectacle!"*

George Balanchine preened himself, replying: *"Cher Maître,* one has done what one can. One has tried to—"

"And the white-faced zany lolling on the staircase," continued the Master. "A touch of genius. A memory of Watteau, with a hint of Schumann. You excel yourself, *mon cher."*

The other checked through his opera-glasses and looked puzzled. But he said nothing.

"I am less happy," resumed Diaghilev, "with the two rather *louche* characters posed to the right of the royal dais. A suggestion of the *commedia dell'arte*, perhaps? You are a waggish fellow, *cher* George."

A baffled silence from his addressee . . .

Down in the orchestra stalls, the sheer, stunning brilliance of Tchaikovsky's music at close quarters had an anaesthetising effect on the brain, but did not in any regard dull that of Liza Carlos, who sat scanning the dancers and the walkers-on through her opera-glasses. Presently, she stiffened and grabbed her companion's arm. "There's Abie and Boris!" she hissed. "Gawd, how do they think they're going to get away with that? Why, they stand out like a couple of pork chops at a bar mitzvah!"

The gloriously colourful *mise en scène* progressed to its climax, with the newly born princess being blessed with all the beauty and graces of this world by the invited fairies, till, with a menacing and sombre note in the score, there appeared the wicked fairy who had not been invited to the junketing. During the exchanges and incantations that followed, anyone could have discerned that Uncle Luigi—in his role of whitefaced zany—was slowly slumping forwards, no doubt on account of the heat, the vibrations, the total éclat. In fact, no one but Ernest Rowbotham noticed it. And grew afraid.

The climax—the screaming imprecations expressively mimed by a supreme artiste, and the dismay of the king, queen and the assembled courtiers—brought the music to its apogee, to total silence. The very short hairs on the back of one's head prickled, and one knew in one's heart, quite suddenly, what art was all about.

And then, out of the silence, which was of the sort that one experiences in one's mind in the timeless blue gloom of Chartres Cathedral, or in St. Mark's Square Venice on a rainy dawn in October, there came the sharp sound of a blow, the noise of flesh striking flesh—followed by a shrill shriek. Shrill, but discernibly male.

And then the stentorian exchange between the two—to quote Diaghilev—*louche* characters to the right of the royal dais:

"What did you have to go and hit that guy for, Boris?"

"Chrissakes, who wants to be groped, in full view of these paying customers, by a fuckin' fairy?"

Very slowly and with infinite grace, Uncle Luigi bowed forward, performed a perfect somersault and descended the stairs, at the foot of which he prostrated himself in an elegant heap.

The curtains swept closed for the end of the scene. It had been a *coup de théâtre* unsurpassed in the history of the Ballets Russes.

CHAPTER 11

Commissaire Paul Darré, having received the confirmation that his wife was indeed carrying twins (and there was also the possibility, it was thought, that there might be triplets), had spent the evening at the Casino, where, having drawn the very last from his bank account—and his last meant that he would be unable to pay the mortgage on his home—had essayed the amount on a single *coup* of trente-et-quarante. This latter game, which does not have the general popularity of roulette, nor ever will, is essentially a rich man's tipple, with maximum stakes twice those of roulette; also it is a simpler game, offering only four basic bets, but the advantage to the bank is marginally less than in roulette. Darré's daring *coup*, which should have doubled his stake, had not come off.

He had progressed a fair way to sinking his misery at the Casino bar counter when his assistant Martin found him out.

"We have trouble here, Chief. Yes, I think I can safely say that we have trouble in Monte Carlo," declared Martin, and with sanguine satisfaction.

"Have a drink," said Darré.

"Well, yes, thanks, Chief," responded the other, a bit put out that his dramatic announcement had not brought forth a more gratifying response. "I'll have what you're having, please."

"All right, what's the trouble?" asked Darré.

"We definitely have Chicago gangsters in town," said Martin. "And they're not just passing through. Following upon the shooting at the Schéhérazade, we have had another incident at the Opera tonight."

Darré showed a gratifying response. "Good God—what happened?"

"Two characters speaking with strong American accents made no less than two attempts to enter the theatre by the stage door. On the first attempt they were roughly ejected by Claude Haquin, the assistant door-keeper—"

"Haquin, I know him well," interposed Darré. "We were at school together. At eleven, he could lift any two of us up on high with both hands outstretched. There was a fellow named—I think his name was Fouchet, and he was killed at Verdun—who conceived the notion of exhibiting Haquin's private parts behind the school bicycle-shed at five centimes a time. He and Haquin cleaned up quite a bit between them, particularly from the girls. Please continue, Martin."

"On the second attempt to enter the theatre," said Martin, "the two produced guns. Sensibly, Haquin, who could have flattened both of them—"

"That he could, that he could!" cried Darré. "What a man! I, too, paid the five centimes to view his appendages, Martin—though I only went along to escort my then current girl friend, one Solange, who put up the money. Do go on."

"Haquin sensibly succumbed to *force majeure* and permitted himself, with the muzzle of a pistol held to his forehead, to be tied hand and foot to the chair in the door-keeper's bothy," said Martin. "The two men then went backstage."

"For what purpose?"

Martin shrugged. "That is a puzzle, Chief. In the event, they went to the dressing-room of"—he consulted his notebook—"Messieurs Anton Repin and Arkadi Surikov. And there they caused these two dancers to remove their costumes, which they then put upon themselves."

"Again I ask, for what purpose, Martin?"

Martin gave another shrug. "Once more, I cannot answer you, Chief. Having left Repin and Surikov bound and gagged in their dressing-room, the two Americans then went on-stage, appearing in the first act of *The Sleeping Beauty*."

"As *dancers*, Martin?"

"Not precisely, Chief. All they were required to do was to stand around and look decorative. I—ah—think that they may have done this with less than the artistry required by the Ballets Russes. In any event, they behaved most appallingly and caused Monsieur Diaghilev to pronounce that the event had never occurred, and was not to be referred to in the press."

"And the view of the Société des Bains de Mer?" Darré was referring to the company that had the franchise on the Principality, and, at the end of the day, on them.

"They are of the same opinion, Chief."

"And? . . ." Darré did no more than gesture westwards, to the promontory upon which stood the palace.

"His Serene Highness is of the same opinion, Chief. In the interests of the Principality, it must not be bruited about that the standards of Chicago gangsterdom have been imported into Monte Carlo."

"Well stated, Martin," responded Commissaire Darré. "Make it so. Rid the Principality of these types. But discreetly. Pick them up. Shovel them across the road into France and let the French police deal with the embarrassment. Why do you tarry, Martin? Drink up your drink and get to work!"

Martin obeyed, and departed, leaving his chief to his personal problems . . .

I wonder, thought Darré, if I could borrow a few hundred francs on the car? Sit in on a game of baccarat with the English nobs, the Indian princes and the like? Win or bust . . .

Which only goes to demonstrate poor Darré's desperation—

for baccarat, what the English call "chemmy," which is short for "chemin de fer," is essentially a millionaires' game, and then only those millionaires with strong nerves.

None but the brave chemin de fer.

Back at the Hôtel de Paris, Liza Carlos changed into a very fetching kimono, built herself a manhattan of densely alcoholic properties and strode up and down her drawing-room, chain-smoking through a cigarette-holder of inconceivable length, pausing at every return to the drinks' table to take another deep sip and occasionally replenish her glass. She kept this up for three hours, till nearly midnight, having quit the theatre immediately after the sensational close of the first act, leaving Larry Rattazini behind to sort out the mess and report back to her.

He phoned at five to twelve.

"What in the hell? . . ." she began.

"It's okay, babe," soothed Rattazini. "Aldo and Poeta got clean away without being challenged. I deemed it prudent—considering that they had burst in and tied up no less than three guys—that they slip over into France for a day or so till the worst of the heat's off. They're now in a small hotel in Cannes right down the road."

"And Luigi?"

"I had it from Aldo and Poeta. Remember that guy who fell down the steps at the finale? That was our guy of the wheelchair. This was why the boys dressed up and tailed him right on to the stage."

"Where is it now?—the thing in the wheelchair?"

"Right back in the hotel. He was delivered back at the stage door and Limey Rowbotham and his frail picked him up in the chauffeured automobile. Ask me why that charade—I can't tell you. Ask me if at any time this guy in the wheelchair was in any way approached, importuned, made to work some kind of switch, and Aldo and Poeta will tell you that he was not. And, finally, for the record, there was no other person of either the male or female persuasion who attended the ballet tonight in a wheelchair. I am on my way back to the hotel, honey. See you soon."

Liza drained the last of her manhattan. "Don't bother to wake me when you return," she said. "I can feel one of my heads coming on."

Ernest and Annabel, having recovered Uncle Luigi from Jean-Pierre (changed, make-up removed, cleaned up generally, and the latter having carried out his commitment to the letter, despite the fact that his assistant had that night been overpowered and trussed up by desperados), returned to the hotel in a quite happy frame of mind. Indeed, they were in very good humour, for the grotesque outburst at the close of the first act, since neither had recognised the two personages involved, had been something to laugh about on the way back. And they both fervently hoped—and stated as much, each to the other—that the shades of Uncle Luigi and his mother had not allowed the fall downstairs to spoil their delight at the spectacle.

They went to bed, and Uncle Luigi to the bathroom. The rigours of the day had quite tired them out, and the joining of hands summed up the low ebb of their mutual passion. Annabel had said that she must go to the hairdresser's in the morning and had indeed fixed an appointment for ten o'clock. At half past nine, after a breakfast of croissants, coffee and kisses, she departed, leaving him in bed to pick his laborious way through a copy of *Le Figaro*—which was full of the collapse of Germany's economic system and of a talking movie featuring the American screen actor Al Jolson—when his bedside phone rang.

"Hello."

"Is that Mr. Rowbotham? This is Nicky. Remember me? The other day we went for a little ride and a little talk. Then you kind of spurned our hospitality and went off with your lady friend. What's her name, . . ."

"Miss Smith," said Rowbotham dully, half of his mind working on an awful possibility.

"Miss Smith—ah. We asked her for her name just now, but she isn't in what you'd call a communicative mood. Are you, Miss Smith?"

Rowbotham brought his fist down upon the telephone table. "You've kidnapped her!" he cried. "See here, you swine—"

"Yes, Mr. Rowbotham?" came the smooth interjection. "You were saying?"

"If you harm a hair of that girl, that lovely girl's head, by golly, I'll—"

"Yes, Mr. Rowbotham, I was sure I had it right. You and little Miss Smith are snookum-dookums. Isn't that nice?"

Rowbotham closed his eyes. "What do you want from me?" he whispered.

"Now that is an inspired question," responded Nicky. "A question like that—though many would think it redundant, not to say tautological—puts us right back into business, to the time when you were answering up quite well at our last meeting, till you tried to hang it on me that Luigi stashed that six million bucks in any old bank. So let us return again to my key question: WHERE IS THE DOUGH HID OUT?"

"I—don't know," breathed Rowbotham. "You must believe me—*I—just—don't—know!*"

"Boys"—the man on the other end had clearly turned his head from the mouthpiece to address his companions in the room—"our friend is suffering yet again from one of his distressing lapses of memory. I think we should maybe help him along a little. Or maybe little Miss Smith could help him along a little—indirectly."

"Don't you touch her!" cried Rowbotham into the mouthpiece, "or so help me, I'll—"

"Help her off with her dress, Boris. My, you do it in the manner born, like you'd been undressing Fifty-second Street chorines all your life."

"Stop it!" howled Rowbotham. "Leave her alone. I don't know where the money is, I tell you!"

"My, my, little Miss Smith ain't so little after all, boys," came the taunting voice. "Who'd like to relieve the lady of her brassiere? You, Elephant? Go right ahead."

"NO!—STOP!—LISTEN TO ME!"

"I think Mr. Rowbotham has maybe had a return of memory, boys," said Nicky. "Go right ahead, Mr. Rowbotham. Meantime, Elephant, you restrain your eager hands."

Rowbotham's brain was darting around in the confines of his skull, trying to attach itself to an idea—any idea. The thought of Annabel in the hands of the four thugs who had threatened him in the canyon, of the unspeakable things they might be contemplating . . .

"Listen," he said, "I'll telephone my uncle's lawyer straight away and have them make a draft of the entire six million available to a bank here in Monte Carlo immediately. How's that?"

"No dice, Mr. Rowbotham," came the response. "Like Luigi would not have trusted his loot to any bank, much less would he have let any shyster lawyers handle anything but small change for you to play ball with in Monte Carlo. That loot is stashed somewhere in portable form, be it in coin, gold, precious stones or the like. If Luigi left that loot to you—and, since he was unable to take it with him where he was going, you are, however unlikely, the candidate—you have to know where it is, or have some clue."

"Please!" pleaded Rowbotham. "I don't—"

"Make with the brassiere, Elephant."

"NO!—LISTEN!"

"Desist for a moment, Elephant, but do not remove your nimble, if revolting, paws from the fastenings. Mr. Rowbotham is having another return of memory."

Rowbotham closed his eyes. There *was* something. Something he had been instructed to do, had done and having done had thrust away into a corner of his mind. But—*which* corner?

"Listen—I . . ."

"Go on, Mr. Rowbotham. No cheating, Elephant. The lady is looking distinctly displeased with you."

"I'VE GOT IT!" shouted Rowbotham.

"He has got it, boys," said Nicky. "Like the romantic soul that I am, I always said that love would find a way. Out with it, Limey—and make it fast this time!"

"Well, almost my first instructions from Uncle Luigi, via his lawyers, after telling me to take the Blue Train down to Monte Carlo and check in at the Hôtel de Paris, was to—it's very odd, but the matter quite slipped my mind till now—"

"Spare me the alibis, bud. The facts. The facts! My boys are wanting Elephant to proceed with this feast of Venus, so that they may continue, and continue and continue . . ."

"No, no—listen!" wailed Rowbotham. "I was instructed to take from my uncle's luggage a lead casket and deposit it in the hotel safe. Which I did."

"This casket. Describe this casket."

"Well, it was made of lead and rather heavy. Shaped like a heart, and—well, the only way to describe it is to say that it looks, in size and shape, like one of those heart-shaped boxes of chocolates that chaps send their sweethearts on Valentine's Day."

"Valentine's Day—aaaaah!"

"Do you think it's significant—that it may contain the—um —loot in some portable form? It was certainly very heavy."

Silence, and then: "Listen to me, Rowbotham, and listen to me but good."

"Yes—er—Nicky."

"Retrieve that casket, that heart-shaped casket, from the hotel safe. Do it now. When you have done so, leave it in full view on the table in the middle of the foyer and return immediately to your room. Got it?"

"Yes, of course," said Rowbotham. "And Annabel—Miss Smith—you'll—"

"Do as you're told, Mr. Rowbotham, and you might—you just *might*—get your snookum-dookums back intact."

The phone went dead.

The general manager himself, no less, escorted Rowbotham down to the vaults where, inside a man-sized safe door that required no less than three keys to open it (each carried jealously by an under-manager), plus a six-letter combination known only to the general manager and changed daily (for the record, on that particular day the word was: "Jolson"), was revealed a veritable mausoleum of smaller safe doors stretching high to the ceiling, all tended by an ancient servitor in a long apron and the sort of bad feet affected by the older generations of Parisian waiters, who produced a long ladder, and, refusing all help, placed it up against the wall of safe doors, whereupon, using the key that Rowbotham had been given upon delivering the lead casket to the hotel's care, produced from out of a repository in the fifth row up the veritable lead casket.

Rowbotham eagerly took the casket, thanked the management, who all bowed deeply in return, and raced up to the lobby, which fortunately was empty. He there deposited the article close by the side of an extremely handsome floral arrangement on the table in the centre of the chamber, in a spot that might be said to have been concealed from most of the passing traffic and certainly from the view of the porters' lodge and Reception. He then darted upstairs.

An hour passed. In that hour, Rowbotham steadfastly did not partake of alcohol, regarding such a digression as offering a hostage to the gods, or a virgin sacrifice to the forces of evil. Around midday, however, he poured himself a large whisky—neat—and stared at it for a considerable time, chin in hand, ruminatively.

"What would I give to have her back?" he asked himself in the Socratic vein. Aloud.

He took the whisky in one swallow, and filled himself another.

"Would I give my right arm?

"Yes, I would give my right arm. Gladly."

He poured another shot and swallowed it down in one.

"Would I give, also, my left arm?

"Yes, I would joyfully give my left arm."

He poured himself another.

"What else would I give to have her back. Now. Immediately? Or at any time?"

The third Scotch he savoured on his tongue, and allowed to slip down in its subtle tartness. "To have her back," he answered himself, "I would give my all, my everything. To see her just once more, I would give all that. To have her, to hold her for evermore, I would give my soul—whatever that is."

The door snicked open on her key. She stood on the threshold. Whipped off a headscarf, preened for him.

"How do you like my new hair-do, darling?" she asked. "The hairdresser, Mademoiselle Angeline, assures me that the shingle and the bandeau are here to stay. Say what you think. Be frank."

He caught her on her second slow pirouette; held her fast, tightly.

"This is wonderful—a miracle!" he breathed into her ear.

"Well, it's only an old hair-do, darling," she said. "Are you all right, Ernest? You sound a little—um—tired and emotional to me."

"Are you all right, Annabel?—are you all right?"

"Why should I not be, darling?" She shook out her shingled hair, smoothed down her new bandeau. "All I've done this morning is sit mostly under a hair-drier and read boring magazines. Oh, sweetie, don't look so lugubrious. You look like someone who's lost a dollar and found a nickel."

He nodded.

"I think I may have lost six million dollars," he said. "But for what I've got back in return—oh, my darling, I don't regret one penny!"

And he held her close.

CHAPTER 12

Nicky Pavese and his boys were sky-high, their joy being adumbrated only by a small set-back, of which later.

They had watched from the stairwell as Ernest Rowbotham had raced—literally raced—to do their bidding; had placed the heart-shaped object on the table in the middle of the foyer and had raced back upstairs to await the safe return of his inamorata, which joyful conjunction, as they knew, could not greatly be delayed, since Boris had tailed Annabel to the hairdresser's and Nicky, at least, was not in ignorance of how long it takes for a lady to come out of such establishments in substantially the same state as that in which she has entered, give or take a couple of curls and a shampoo that she could have fixed in her own handbasin at a fiftieth of the cost.

"We have it, boys!" declared Nicky, patting the heart-shaped casket. "This is indubitably IT!"

"Diamonds, or the like?" ventured Abie.

"Undoubtedly," responded his ringleader. "As was the case with Chuck O'Brien when he cashed in his proceeds and flitted to Valparaiso with that frail from Minsky's. Or when Ralph Sheldon, thinking that Capone was going to move in on him, decided to go liquid, bought up a cache of diamonds and emeralds from Rube Levy—you remember Rube?"

"Rube I remember well," supplied Abie. "I was at his bar mitzvah and he at mine. I was also at his funeral. For helping out Sheldon, Al should not have been so spiteful."

"It is always Al's way."

"Yes."

"Well," said Nicky Pavese, "to settle any doubts, we will open it up, and that should present no problem. Give me your knife, Boris."

Boris produced the requisite item: a clasp-knife with a thick, wickedly curved blade that could have scalped a rhinoceros. It made no impression whatsoever upon the lead casket, give or take a couple of light scratches.

"A can-opener, maybe?" suggested Abie.

"Ring down to room service for one," said Nicky. "This is ridiculous, that we should have six million bucks in our hands yet be unable to pay this goddamned hotel bill."

The bill in question—the small set-back to which already referred—had been presented with their breakfast tray. Astronomical in magnitude, including as it did the cost of the champagne and caviar that the quartette had consumed, with the aid of four ladies of the town, during their alfresco party the previous evening, it also carried with it the hard cutting-edge of a curt note from the general manager requesting immediate payment. This was undoubtedly on account of the complaints that had been received about the party.

In due course, a waiter arrived with a can-opener. On a silver tray. When he had gone, Elephant set to upon the lead casket. And got nowhere at all.

"In my opinion, Nicky," said Elephant at length. "Dis is what I tink—"

"Let nobody move!" cried Nicky. "Lock all the doors! No one to leave or enter! The oracle is about to deliver! Give, Elephant."

The giant's homely countenance was suffused with the pink of pure pleasure. "Tanks, Nicky," he said. "And dis is my opinion, dat what we have here is not like you might compare with a can of beans." He picked up the casket in his massive hands and jockeyed with its weight. "I am tinking dat maybe we are trying to get into lead which is maybe two inches or more."

Nicky smacked his brow. "Elephant's mighty brain has penetrated further than that of us lesser mortals," he declared. "Of course, Luigi would not consign six million smackers' worth of precious stones into a mere bean can. What we have here, my friends, is a veritable miniature safe. So how do we crack it? I am open to ideas from the floor of the house."

"Find a garage or a small engineering plant and have them open it up with a blowtorch or something," subscribed Abie.

"So then out pours six millions' worth of precious stones," said Nicky. "How are we going to explain this to the guys in this garage or small engineering plant?"

"We could rub them out," suggested Boris.

"And bring down upon our heads another whole load of trouble," responded his ringleader. "Boys, this is not Chicago. We have no protection here. No one has been fixed. We have expended no moolah on squaring the cops and the judiciary. We walk naked in these streets." He strode the length of the room and back again. "Ideas, ideas!" he chanted. "Gimme ideas!"

"Um—we could go someplace else, where we got friends, Nicky," suggested Elephant.

Nicky Pavese snapped his fingers. Brightened. Pointed.

"Again we have the touch of genius!" he declared. "Praise the Lord that you have lived to see this day, Elephant. Friends! That's it! *Sicily!*"

"*Sicily?*" The others chorused.

"Don't I have no less than five brothers and three sisters living just across the water there?" said Nicky. "Not to mention nieces and nephews innumerable, and that's not taking into account more aunts and uncles than you'd believe. And one of the latter—Uncle Mario—*is the village blacksmith!*"

"How we get to Sicily, Nicky?"

"How we get outa this goddamned hotel without paying the bill?"

Nicky waved aside their doubts. "We will fly to Sicily," he declared. "As to getting out of the hotel, we will walk out, one by one, casually, like we was going out to buy a newspaper or a cigar at the corner store."

"We are going to look pretty strange going out casually to buy a newspaper carrying a violin case," observed Abie. "And that's not to mention the double-bass case. Plus the rest of the baggage."

Nicky smote his brow. "You have it right," he said. "Maybe we shall have to abandon the baggage and the artillery to the more important issue of getting this hunk of lead to Sicily, where my Uncle Mario will carve it open in his blacksmith's shop."

"Um, we could lower da stuff outa da window, Nicky," interposed Elephant. "We're only two floors up, and we could make a rope by tying bedsheets together, like I once saw on da movies."

Nicky spread his hands. "What can I say?" he asked. "In the light of such genius, I can only stand and stare.

"Get to work with the bedsheets, boys!"

The departure of the Nicky Pavese gang from the august portals of the Hôtel de Paris passed almost unregarded—but not entirely.

The initial part of the operation, that is to say the casual exit of three members of the consortium on their way to purchase fictitious newspapers and cigars, went off very well; none of the trio was challenged by the hall staff. Elephant, remaining behind to lower down the baggage and the instrument cases (their suite was at the rear of the great hotel, overlooking a quiet alley-way), similarly carried out his task; the gear was picked up by the others and taken along to a cab-rank half a block away. It only remained for Elephant to get out and join them.

Alas . . . alas . . .

Half-way across the sumptuous foyer, close by Louis Quatorze on his prancing charger with the polished kneecap, Elephant chanced to drop a small item of his personal chattels, to wit a plug of Old Andy's Rum-Matured Chewing Tobacco, the loss of which he did not perceive. However, a keen-eyed page, a youth in buttoned livery, saw the packet fall, picked it up and ran after the giant, who, no sooner had he got out of the door than he broke into a smart trot, to join his companions at the cab-rank.

The youth quickened his pace to match.

"M'sieu! M'sieu!" he cried. "Vous avez laissé tomber quelque chose!"

The well-meant information that he had dropped something, delivered as it was in a language of which he was totally ignorant, served only to increase the rate of the giant's flight. One glance over his shoulder was enough to tell him that his pursuer wore the livery of the Hôtel de Paris, and that, though small in stature, he had a red and determined-looking face.

"M'sieu! M'sieu—arrêtez!"

There was no stopping Elephant, who thought the game was up and that the hue and cry had been raised on account of them attempting a midday moonlight flit. Rounding the block, he came in sight of his companions, who were loading the gear aboard a waiting cab.

"Get this guy off my back!" shouted Elephant. "I tink he must be heading up a posse!"

A posse!

"Get out the Equaliser, Boris!" snapped Nicky Pavese. "Blast that little guy and anyone who's following after him."

The double-bass case was opened and the Thompson taken

out, contingent upon which the cab driver began to weep and plead (in French) that he had a wife and seven children and they could have every sou he had in the kitty and the vehicle besides. He was ignored.

Boris cocked the sub-machine-gun, took hasty aim to the left of Elephant and loosed off a trial burst to get the range right. The slugs struck the wall close by the buttoned page and streaked past his ear, whereupon the lad, whose devotion to duty did not run to expending his life on account of a pack of chewing tobacco, dropped the latter and ducked down an alley-way that was conveniently near.

Elephant gained the cab, leapt aboard with the rest. Boris laid the muzzle of the Thompson lovingly against the cab driver's ear.

"Airport, bud," he said. "*Compree?*"

"*Oui, m'sieu—oui!*" bleated the other.

The hue and cry was, indeed, swiftly raised, for the page-boy, not even wasting time by telephoning, ran two blocks to police headquarters and was soon blurting out his news to Commissaire Darré and Sergeant Martin, with elegances like descriptions of the four men and the number of the cab, which he last saw heading in the direction of Nice. Both police officers commended him.

"Get after them, Martin," said Darré. "I'll telephone Nice and have them set up a road-block. They won't get far, never fear. These are our Chicago gangsters who shot the type from Orange and his whore. If we can contrive to let the French police make the actual arrests, they'll all be guillotined and we shall be spared a lot of paper work. So don't strive too strenuously to catch up with them."

"Right, Chief." Martin was—not surprisingly—relieved to be given the direct order that he was not to close with the quartette of machine-gun-toting desperados. He departed in the second-fastest police car they had, along with a couple of uniformed men armed with single-shot carbines that were relics of the Crimean War.

Darré watched them go, shrugged, put through the call to Nice and went back to his paper work—which he had slipped under his blotter upon the arrival of the excited page-boy of the Hôtel de Paris. This consisted of a complicated system for breaking the bank at Monte Carlo devised by Lord Rosslyn, which, apart from calling for a large capital (which, in his desperation, Darré was hoping to raise by taking out another mortgage on his house), also required, in his lordship's telling phrase: "perseverance, strong nerves and the constitution of a dray-horse."

In the event, and greatly to his advantage, Martin never came within sight of the runaways. Upon approaching the Anglican church, the police car was halted for half an hour by the traffic and milling throng attendant upon the nuptials of the gallant British admiral and his handsome widow from Boston, Massachusetts, Mrs. Willibrand, by special licence granted by the Bishop of Gibraltar, in whose See the Principality lies. Mrs. Willibrand, who not only owned a steam yacht of thirteen hundred gross tonnage that was more or less permanently aground in Monte Carlo harbour on a bed of empty champagne bottles and caviar pots, but also had one of the finest villas in Cap d'Ail down the coast, and had done some hefty entertaining during her brief but whirlwind courtship with the British sea-dog, including all those luminaries with whom they had travelled down on the Blue Train, notably Mr. Gordon Selfridge and the Dolly sisters, the five-times-divorced Argentinian heiress, the Scottish laird (who had *not* made the same kind of running with the former as the admiral had with the Bostonian widow) and simply *all* the *bon ton* of the Riviera, my dear. All had been sent an invitation to the wedding; all save the French marquis whose ancestor had died in the arms of St. Louis—and would not have been seen dead at an affair so parvenu—had accepted. Hence the halting of the Monégasque police pursuit.

Much to the relief of Martin and his carbine-toting aides.

Annabel, whose brief concerning Uncle Luigi's fortune had not included information as to how and in what currency, portable or otherwise, that fortune stood, conceded that it might, indeed, be carried within the lead casket and that Ernest could well have given it away for love of her and for her chastity. Not herself a Chicagoan, she had nevertheless some insight into the ways of the gangsters and conceived it quite likely that Uncle Luigi's loot might well have been in the liquid form of precious gems—knowing the racketeers' aversion to the banking system.

So overcome was she by Ernest's sacrifice on her imagined behalf that she felt constrained to express her reciprocal passion. This kept them in bed till nearly two o'clock, and with no luncheon.

Commissaire Darré, in the meantime, had had a telephone message from his mortgage company informing him that they deemed it impossible, in view of his greatly reduced assets, to grant a further advance upon his property. (In fact, so closed-in is the world of the Principality that the fact of the Commissaire of Police gambling heavily on the tables had been fed back to them.) Hardly had he digested this sideswipe than Martin rang up from Nice to say that the gangsters had escaped them, the road-block not having been set up. The fact was that the Nice police had no more fancy for tackling heavily armed gangsters than their colleagues in Monte Carlo, so they had telephoned ahead to the police at Orange to set up a road-block—meanly omitting to mention the Thompson-machine-gun factor.

But by this time, Nicky Pavese and his boys were in a

quiet corner of Nice airport, negotiating for a charter flight to Sicily.

Every newly burgeoning airport, in the halcyon days of the Blue Train, contained within its perimeter the raffish and ramshackle evidence of extremely private enterprise: ex-pilots and observers of the Great War who had sunk their savings into ex-war-planes and converted them into passenger-and-goods-carrying craft, and this in the days when such safety regulations as applied were seldom observed save in the breach.

To such a set-up did Nicky Pavese direct their cab driver: to a promising-looking conglomerate of hangar and ticky-tacky lean-to in one of the most remote corners of the field. Parked outside the hangar was a twin-engined biplane that must in its time have carried bombs, but now bore the legend emblazoned upon its fuselage:

Compagnie Aéronautique de Gaspard

The cab driver they dismissed, to his tremendous relief. And furthermore they paid his due, with a tip on the side. But the quite specific threats concerning his future capability of procreation should he ever breathe a word about the manner of their departure he took entirely to heart.

"*Bonjour, messieurs*—Americans, yes?"

The speaker was a diminutive creature in a leather coat, riding-breeches and high boots, sporting a rakish moustache, a kepi cap worn exaggeratedly over one ear and a black eye patch. He was also puffing on a long thin cigar.

"Yes," responded Nicky. "We want to go to Sicily. Today. Now. As of this moment."

"That will be easy," came the response. "To Sicily I fly often. *O sole mio*"—he sang a couple of bars, choked on his cigar. "Payment in advance," he declared. "And that will be" —he named a fair price that did not greatly strain the gang's liquidity. Nicky Pavese paid it over there and then.

"My name is Capitaine Fulke de Gaspard," declared the aviator. "Formerly of the *la célèbre escadrille des Cigognes*, comrade of Guynemer, Nungesser, Bourjade, Madon, Pinsard, Fonck (a great *ami* of mine, René), Boyau, Coiffard. I knew them all. Twenty-five victories against the Boche, me. We gave them hell. My last Spad, she is a civic monument in my home town, still riddled with the bullets of my last engagement. He hiccuped. "I think that we must have a drink together before *le départ*, yes? Follow me." He led them towards the ticky-tacky lean-to.

The gang looked at each other. Nicky Pavese shrugged his shoulders. They followed after the French aviator and self-declared war ace.

"The fortune having departed," said Ernest Rowbotham, "the whole apparatus of Uncle Luigi's will has gone with it, as far as I can see, together with the interest of the Dogs' Home, which you represent, darling." It seemed odd, after a lifelong celibacy that had ceased two nights previously, to be calling someone "darling," he thought.

"I quit from the Dogs' Home as of today," replied Annabel. "Sent off the wire just as soon as you told me what you'd done about the lead casket. We're free, darling—free!"

"All save for—him," said Ernest, pointing to Uncle Luigi, who, out of delicacy, they had turned towards the wall during their extended dalliance. "And we really can't dump him just like a heap of garbage, can we, Annabel?"

"Hardly, darling," said she, "after all, he could be said to have brought us together."

They kissed.

The door burst open.

On the threshold stood Liza Carlos, in a stunning afternoon frock by Worth of Paris, with a cloche hat made of enough bird-of-paradise feathers surely to have put at hazard the continuation of the species. Beside her was Larry Rattazini. He carried a pistol. When he saw the state of the two in the bed, he grinned and slipped the weapon back into his shoulder-holster. Annabel covered her bare breasts with her hands; Ernest made some shift to cover them both with the sheets.

"Where is Luigi Gaudi?" demanded Liza, in the voice of an Assyrian queen condemning to death a thousand captives.

Rowbotham pointed to the mute figure in the hat which sat facing the wall opposite. He put a protective arm around Annabel, who was trembling and beginning to weep.

"You can have him," he said. "If he's any use to you, I beg you to take him away, Miss—er—Mrs. . . ."

Liza Carlos strode over to the wheelchair and spun it around, so that the figure faced her; which done, she whipped off the hat; next, after a pause of distaste, she tore off the mask, revealing the hideous face, the rictus grin, the lips crudely sewn and oversewn with coarse black cotton.

"This isn't Luigi Gaudi," she declared, and there was an overtone of sadness in her voice. "I knew Luigi well, though not for long, and no guy who looked as wonderful as he could possibly have been reduced to this, I am telling you. Why, when *this* thing was alive, he was an old guy. Luigi was *my* age, maybe a year or two younger and all the broads he met had hots for him. This proves my point, Larry—Luigi is still alive and . . ."

While she was speaking, the door had quietly opened behind her back and that of her companion—the living one. Ernest and Annabel saw the newcomer quite clearly from where they lay in the bed, arms about each other.

The newcomer was that genial player of the tables, Ezekiel Bragg. Unaccountably, the short hairs at the nape of Ernest's neck prickled and stiffened at the sight of him.

"Hi, Liza. Long time no see. This is your old friend Luigi."

CHAPTER 13

It was Larry Rattazini who first reacted, and with commendable alacrity. His hand was groping for his gun even as he turned. It froze there, under his armpit, when an automatic appeared as if by magic in the other man's hand.

Liza Carlos backed up against the wall for support, pressing her knuckles against her mouth, choking back a scream. It was quite a while before she spoke, and the man by the door continued to smile at her.

"You have to be Luigi Gaudi," she said presently, "if only because no one else in all Chicago was ever able to pull a gun that fast. But—I don't understand . . ."

The man known to Ernest as Zeke Bragg was still smiling as he lightly touched his cheek. "The face?" he said. "Plastic surgery, Liza, done by the best operator on the East Coast. Then there was a specialist in Detroit who made a couple of nicks in my larynx that sent my voice down half an octave, so that even my own mama wouldn't have known me over the telephone." The smile faded as he switched his gaze to Larry Rattazini. The scarfaced man backed away another pace from the gun that was still aimed at him. "You didn't blast me in Pauli's that day, rat," said Luigi Gaudi. "I'd been tipped off by a squealer in your mob, so I went someplace else for lunch." He gestured towards the mute figure in the chair. "So you got that poor bastard, who spent the rest of his life in a wheelchair, looking at comic books and girlie magazines and dreaming of what might have been on the Riviera."

"Then—who? . . ." Liza gestured towards the mute figure.

"Beppo Mazzini," said the other. "In his day, he was a useful small-timer—making the collections, driving get-away cars, that kind of small change. Beppo never amounted to much, but he took the shots for me that day in Pauli's, and I more or less set him up: told him to take my seat at the table. He never knew that I'd set him up."

Out of the long silence that followed, Ernest Rowbotham somehow found his voice . . .

"And you salved your conscience by indulging him, er . . ."

The lips under the handsome moustache curled in a smile of pure affection. "Call me Uncle Luigi, dear boy," he said. "Yes, that's what I did. I indulged the poor old bastard, fixed the whole thing the way he wanted it. But, before we go any further into the details"—he turned to Larry Rattazini, who flinched away—"take out your gun, rat, and take it out real slow, holding it by the end of the butt, with your fingers well away from the trigger. Hold it like you were picking up a scorpion by its tail. And then drop it on the floor."

Rattazini obeyed.

"Luigi, don't shoot him!" cried Liza.

"Would I be so stupid, Liza?" responded Luigi Gaudi. "Here—in the Hôtel de Paris? And after I've covered up my tracks so well? No, rat"—returning his attention to the shrinking man—"I'm not jeopardizing all my well-laid plans for the pleasure of bumping *you* off. Do you have the fare back to the States?"

"Yeah, yeah, I do—um—Luigi," admitted the other, with hope dawning in his eyes.

"Then move it, rat," said Luigi Gaudi, "before I change my mind and blast you out of pure inertia. And listen here, rat . . ."

"Yes—um—Luigi?"

"When you get back to Chicago—when you get back to Chicago"—the clever, bright eyes gleamed with a visionary light—"tell them all about Luigi Gaudi. Tell Touhy and O'Banion. Tell Bugs Moran, Guilfoyle, Druggan, Ralph Sheldon, Spike O'Donnell. But most of all tell Al. Al most of all.

"Tell them how Luigi outsmarted them all. How he lived to tell the tale and got away with his loot.

"Don't stint yourself, rat. Tell all. By the time you shoot off your mouth, Luigi Gaudi will have vanished from the scene for ever, and you wouldn't find him any more than you'd find a guy named Aloysius Ponsonby Macahenny by standing in State Street on a Saturday night and accosting every passer-by.

"Now—move it, rat!"

Rattazini moved himself without a backward glance to anyone.

Ernest Rowbotham cleared his throat. His uncle glanced at him with indulgent affection.

"You were about to make an announcement, dear boy?" he suggested.

"Er—you aren't going to like this very much—er—Uncle Luigi," said Ernest.

"Try it on me, dear boy," responded the other, still smiling.

"Well, there's this other gang of chaps led by a fellow named Nicky."

"Nicky Pavese, I know him well. It has always been my ambition to attend the funerals of him and his three followers —with the added pleasure of having been the agency that set in train those sad obsequies. But do continue, dear boy."

"Well—er . . ."

"I'll tell him, darling," said Annabel.

And she did: how his nephew had sacrificed the six million dollars for her modesty and chastity.

When she had finished, Uncle Luigi laughed lightly. "Have you read your instructions for today?" he asked.

"Well, no, actually we haven't," admitted Ernest. "We've been—ah—rather busy."

"Then read them now, dear boy," suggested his uncle.

Hugging his private parts, Ernest got out of bed and padded over to the chest of drawers, from which he extracted the sealed envelope relating to the current day, the day in question.

"Open it and read it, dear boy," said his uncle.

And Ernest did; with Uncle Luigi smiling all the while; with Annabel huddled nude and wide-eyed under the sheets; and Liza Carlos, no less wide-eyed, wondering what fate was open to her.

Dear Nephew Ernest,
I have lived a bad life, but my heart has always stayed in the place where I was born. In innocence. What I want you to do for me now is this. I want for you to take my heart back where it belongs. My body—nothing. My heart—my all. I want for you to take the lead casket, where mortician Weinberg will have put it after the embalming, and throw it into the sea off Sicily. Well out. Where it won't be washed ashore and somebody use the lead casket as a doorstop. Do this for me, Nephew Ernest.

Yours ever,
Uncle Luigi.

"Oh, God!" cried Ernest, "I gave them his heart. The heart that he wanted to be buried off the shore of Sicily."

"Oh, Ernest!" Annabel was crying. Careless of her nudity, she had reached for her handbag and taken out her own copy of the instructions. "How could we have done this to him?"

Her mind working like an abacus, Liza Carlos addressed her sometime lover:

"Then where *is* the loot, Luigi?" she demanded, eyes blazing with more than rapaciousness as she regarded him.

Luigi Gaudi smiled, pointed to the figure in the wheelchair:

"Inside *him*," he replied. "Where it has been all this while—in the place where his guts used to be before the embalmment. Sure, as Nephew Ernest said, I salved my conscience by indulging Beppo's last wishes, but the poor old guy performed his last and faithful service for me by smuggling six million dollars' worth of uncut diamonds into Europe without paying a cent of Customs' duty." He grinned at Ernest. "You can imagine how I felt when I found him sitting around in the street the other day—all alone."

"Ah, it was *you* who brought him back here!" exclaimed Ernest.

"Who else, dear boy?"

Luigi Gaudi had the delicacy to wheel the corpse into the bathroom to perform his gruesome task. He emerged quite soon with a leather bag about the size of a wash-bag, the kind that carries soap, face-flannel, tooth-brush and toothpaste, that kind of thing. The bag was riddled with holes. When Gaudi laid it on the console table near the bed, he had no need to unfasten the neck of the bag to display the contents; they streamed out: ten or twelve uninspiring chunks of smooth stone, irregularly shaped, dullish yellow-white in colour, varying in size from that of a sparrow's egg to one—spectacularly larger—the size of a duck's egg.

"Good God!" exclaimed Ernest.

"Did you say something, dear boy?" asked his uncle.

"Well, yes," said Ernest. "I've been picking those things up off the carpet ever since that night when Uncle Luigi—that's to say Beppo—was hit. I must have found at least three."

"I'm not surprised, dear boy," responded his relation. "Those slugs didn't improve Beppo any. Might one ask what you did with the uncut diamonds that you—in your own words—picked up from the carpet?"

"I—ah—dropped them into the waste-paper basket," whispered Ernest.

His indulgent uncle merely shrugged. "You win a little, you lose a little," he responded. "There is still more here than I shall need to keep me in the pink, as they say, all my life. And I'm telling you, dear boy, that I have worked for this. After dear Liza's torpedo took the shots at poor old Beppo, and I also had the news that Al and others had decided that Luigi was too good to be true and had to be taking more than his share of the action (and they were right, for I'd been milking everyone else's territories for years, and nobody suspected, not right till the end, nobody suspected Luigi, Mr. Nice Guy), I took the advantage of the situation, let it be known that I was stuck in a wheelchair for life, and continued to run my operations from the background with a new name, a new face and using various front men—among whom, it has to be said, there was a very high mortality rate. What it cost me in floral tributes!"

"You are a bastard, Luigi!" hissed Liza Carlos, who had been listening to this peroration with mounting ire. "A bastard!"

"Why are you beefing, babe?" responded the other. "I gave you the best week of my life, and incidentally also relieved you of your repulsive spouse, and that must have been a relief."

Liza burst into tears. He passed her a handkerchief.

"To revert to my loot, dear boy," said Luigi, addressing his nephew. "I apologise for having deceived you, but you have

The Man Who Broke the Bank at Monte Carlo 165

had what you English would call a rattling good holiday"—he glanced at Annabel Smith and raised an eyebrow—"so you have nothing to complain about. Moreover, when I finally depart this Vale of Tears, everything that I own—and it is considerable—I shall will to you."

"That's very kind of you, Uncle," said Ernest.

Luigi Gaudi picked up the largest of the stones, the one the size of a duck's egg, and regarded it.

"This uncut diamond, dear boy, I have on good authority, will render a perfect, pear-shaped gem of over seventy carats, making it among the fifty or so largest diamonds in the world. When those Amsterdam diamond-cutters have finished their work, nephew mine, this stone alone will be worth four million dollars. The rest"—he gestured to the smaller stones heaped on the table—"will possibly be worth twice that amount when they have been cut. Not a bad investment, you will think."

Liza Carlos had finished crying, but she retained the handkerchief.

"What's going to happen to me?" she asked plaintively. "My mob's all busted up. By the time Larry Rattazini's spread it around, I shall be the laughing-stock of Chicago after what's happened here." She dabbed her nose with the handkerchief.

"Honey," said Luigi Gaudi, "I am now departing. I have nothing in the world but the suit I stand up in, a tailcoat, some loose change—and a potential twelve million dollars. If you want to come with me, you're welcome."

"Coming?"

When Liza flew into his arms, it was Annabel who burst into tears and had to be comforted. All round, it was a distinctly emotional and lachrymose occasion, but with overtones of some joy. Eyes were dabbed. Noses were blown. Kisses were exchanged and hands shaken.

"Uncle, what am I going to do about? . . ." Ernest pointed to the bathroom.

"Beppo is *your* problem, dear boy," responded his uncle. "And I am confident that you will deal with him real fine." He was about to leave, his arm still around the lachrymose and emotional Liza, when an idea occurred to him. From his pocket, he took a billfold of French francs and tossed it on the bed.

"Something on account from your future inheritance, dear boy," he said. "Stake it on black and number thirteen, and do it thirteen times. Thirteen was always my lucky number, likewise black my lucky colour. So long."

They were gone.

Ernest and Annabel looked at each other. He trailed a finger down her cheek and caught a small tear that, expressed from the corner of her eye, had mounted the perfection of her cheekbone and was descending.

"Don't be sad, darling," he said. "Everything has turned out for the best. Uncle Luigi and his lady friend—well—they're probably not much by most people's standards of morality and so forth, but they're obviously stuck on each other. Good luck to them."

"I'm not crying for them," she said, "but for poor Uncle Luigi—and I shall never be able to think of him as any other than Uncle Luigi—and how his greatest wish (and I'm sure it was his greatest wish, more than the Casino, the *thé dansant*, the night-club and all) was to have his heart buried off the coast of Sicily. And we've let him down."

"As the real Uncle Luigi said," responded Ernest, "'You win a little, you lose a little.' One can't get it right all the time. But I tell you what . . ." He sat up on one elbow and faced her, close.

"What?"

"Tonight, we are going to break the bank at Monte Carlo!" He picked up the roll of notes.

"I'll wear my black chiffon. And my engagement ring, which I had to pay for myself, but which will do till you can afford to buy me one, darling."

"And we'll take Uncle Luigi—the hell, let's continue to call him Uncle Luigi."

"Of course—of course. He'll love it."

The Great War bomber droned grandly over the northern tip of Corsica. Capitaine de Gaspard, who flew by the simplistic school of navigation, eschewing charts, altered course somewhat to the left to keep the Italian mainland in sight, a bank of heat haze having grown up since they had left Nice. He took a swig of absinthe from the glass that stood at his elbow. Elba lay to his left. Beyond, the islet of Giglio. Beyond that, the blue waste of the Tyrrhenian Sea, Rome, Naples and Sicily.

He sang—and for the umpteenth time:

"O sole mio . . ."

His voice came back very clearly to his four passengers, who sat in makeshift deck-chairs in the narrow fuselage to the rear.

"In my opinion," stated Abie, "that guy is stoned right out of his mind. Rather than have him flying this aeroplane I would have my mother, who never drove anything faster or more dangerous than a carpet-sweeper."

"I am inclined to the same view," conceded Nicky Pavese, "particularly having seen him sink a whole half bottle of that gut-rot back at the airfield. However, I am reminded that one of the best get-away drivers of my experience—I speak of Bernie Sacco—you will recall Bernie, Boris."

"Yes, yes," agreed the latter, "for didn't I serve a stretch with Bernie, and afterwards kept house with his sister, who once carried booze for a speak-easy on West Sixty-third Street? Man, that frail could carry, would you believe?—six bottles of hooch in a kind of sash around her middle, under her coat. Mamie was her name."

The aeroplane gave a lurch in an air pocket, nearly awakening Elephant, who had lolled in his chair with his great head bowed ever since they left Nice.

"Reverting to Bernie Sacco," said Nicky Pavese, "Bernie, he never went into a job without he had at least a quart of liquor inside him. No, I don't tell a lie. With Bernie, I went on more jobs than I could count. In and out. Blam, blam! Whether it was a bootlegging job or a shoot-out, or whatever, us guys would pile out of the joint shooting as we went, and there would be Bernie out front, the engine revving, his foot on the clutch. We'd be in. Wham! And off we'd go. I never knew another guy who could get around Chicago like he could, drunk or sober. Wrong way up the one-way streets, up on the sidewalks and down alley-ways that looked like they went to no place but put you right back on the main highway. And all done when drunk. Man, after some of the jobs we did, and a get-away that should be written on tablets, we would lift Bernie Sacco out of the driver's seat and carry him up to bed legless. Legless, I tell you!"

From up front came the refrain:

"*La donna è mobile* . . ."

Commissaire Darré felt rather better than he had for quite a while. For a start, he had received a call from his opposite number across the road in France, to the effect that two characters, by name Aldo Ricasoli and Poeta Minghetti, had been picked up on suspicion of being vagrants. In support of their *not* being vagrants, Ricasoli and Minghetti had asserted that they were booked in at the Hôtel de Paris, contingent upon which Darré had had a search made of their suite. In it was found the small wooden crate containing books and other items (including a model, by Messrs. Hornby Trains of England, of the Blue Train), together with a cache of arms and ammunition. Questioned later, the pair admitted to having brought the crate through Customs at Le Havre, where the presence of the train set and other items had so charmed the Customs officer that he had refrained from probing deeper into the chest and discovering its false bottom. Darré was pleased with the outcome: two of the Chicago gangsters had been captured—and not on his territory. He could now devote himself, with a clear mind, to his *problem* . . .

Lord Rosslyn's "infallible system" still commending itself to him, but lacking the funds to support it, Darré had appealed to a maiden aunt of his—a lady of uncertain years who lived in a small villa in Menton—to lend him fifty thousand francs, on the pretext that one of the children needed an urgent and expensive operation on her eyes. To such devices are desperate men driven. The aunt, brought to tears by the plight of the child—her favourite—immediately withdrew all her savings derived from her pension as a war widow and pressed them into her nephew's hand. Darré, who was a good man at heart, but sorely driven beyond his wits' end to salvage his liquidity, his property, his job, reputation, even (remembering the old service revolver in the locked drawer of his desk) his very life, suffered no pang of conscience when he took the money—only heartfelt relief.

He laid out the fifty thousand on his desk, and referred again to Lord Rosslyn's system, which is based on a progression, so that after each *coup* one enhances one's stake by a unit, and increases or decreases the same depending upon one's losses or winnings. It still looked good to Darré.

He glanced at his pocket watch: three o'clock. By now the afternoon session in the *salles privées* would be well under way, with the well-heeled of Europe, the Americas and the

Indian subcontinent throwing away maximum stakes as if there were no tomorrow.

Well, he would join them. Aunt Angélique's loan would—granting that Lord Rosslyn was right—save everything.

Or else—and he glanced towards the locked drawer of his desk—there would be no tomorrow. Not for him.

The clatter of the ex-bomber's twin engines and the hot sunlight shining in through the small and grimy windows, together with the total lack of fresh air, reduced the four passengers to a torpidity of which Elephant's had early been the model.

Up front, Capitaine de Gaspard, inspired by the brilliant Italian coastline far away on his left and also by the half-empty bottle of absinthe on his right, continued to give out with the airs of the South, with snatches from *Rigoletto,* from *Tosca, Aïda, Cavalleria Rusticana, Pagliacci* and many more.

Nicky Pavese, his head slumped against the side of the cabin, and in close contact with the body politic of the machine, was the first of the quartette to detect certain minute changes of tone and tempi in the engines, an occasional hesitation, a misfire, a splutter here and there. He—dreaming of how, when his uncle the blacksmith had opened up Luigi Gaudi's lead casket, he was going to settle down in his native village near Palermo, buy the *castello* from the impoverished lord of the manor, the *marchese,* and wed the latter's snooty daughter, that village beauty who had never so much as treated the young, barefoot Nicky to a glance—woke up immediately the sound of the engines stopped, and there was a great silence.

Boris woke up too. "We're here, I guess," he declared, and looked out of the grimed window, not to see the parched earth of Sicily, but the wrinkled blue wavelets of the Tyrrhenian Sea around a thousand feet below.

"What the hell's going on?" demanded Nicky Pavese.

He was soon answered. Capitaine de Gaspard appeared at the cut-out in the bulkhead leading to the cockpit. Kepi still at a rakish angle, jaunty as ever, a smile on his face.

"Alas, gentlemen," he announced, "I forgot to fill up with gasoline before leaving Nice. We nearly made it, but not quite.

"*Tant pis—c'est la vie!*"

The aeroplane, powerless, unguided, went into a stall and dived the thousand feet into the shimmering blueness.

Away on the horizon, rising from the heat haze, was the humped shape of Etna, highest mountain in Sicily.

The heart of Beppo—alias Uncle Luigi—had come home.

CHAPTER 14

It could be said that Annabel Smith felt brilliant when she entered the *salles privées* that evening at about seven on the arm of Ernest Rowbotham; she in her black chiffon evening frock that displayed to tremendous advantage her long and tapering legs and other attributes, with the diamond ring of her first and fruitless essay into matrimony twinkling like a small segment of the Milky Way on the third finger of her left hand; he in tuxedo, with Uncle Luigi's advance upon his inheritance tucked into his breast pocket. After them came the spurious Uncle Luigi, propelled in his chair by the faithful Charles.

"*Messieurs, faites vos jeux.*" The time-honoured injunction of the croupier was as one with the colour and the dazzle of expensive frocks and jewellery, the heady scent of exclusive perfume and the reek of Havana cigars, the occasional subtle aromatic tang of a dark red carnation worn in the buttonhole of the discerning, the click-click of the ball as it made its descent, the sudden hush of silence, the raising of many hopes, the total indifference of the few to whom the act of actually *losing* money was the sole—and frequently orgasmic—reason for them being there in the first place.

"*Les jeux sont faits, rien ne va plus.*"

"We'll play this table, darling," said Rowbotham. "This is where I made the first bet of my life and it came off."

"I saw you do it, darling," responded she. "I was right over there taking notes of every move you made."

There was a chap seated by them: a stocky individual with a stubbly moustache, dressed in a tuxedo. He had a single forty-franc plaque which he was passing from one hand to the other, his eyes fixed upon the green baize, yellow-marked table in front of him, irresolute. He gave a start as Rowbotham touched him on the shoulder.

"Excuse me, sir. Do you mind if my companion and I take two adjacent seats and you move down one?"

It was a reasonable request and it was reasonably and civilly acceded to. The chap moved to the next chair, Rowbotham took the one he had vacated, Annabel sat alongside her lover and Charles the chauffeur pushed Uncle Luigi into the space beyond her.

"Right!" said Rowbotham. "We go maximum on thirteen and black, and keep it up for thirteen spins of the wheel—and I feel in my heart that we simply can't lose."

Everyone else was laying their bets. The stocky individual next to Rowbotham said: "Excuse me, monsieur, I cannot help but notice that you are playing maximum stakes. Do you perhaps have a system, or are you, as we say, playing off the top of your head?"

"A bit of both, sir," responded Rowbotham. "Here goes."

"*Rien ne va plus,*" called the croupier, shortly followed by: "*Treize, noir, impair et pair.*"

The deft croupier, having dragged in the losings with his little rake, shoved a considerable pile of chips in Rowbotham's direction, double for his *chance simple* on black, thirty-five times his stake on thirteen.

"Oh, Ernest!" cried Annabel. "I'm so happy."

They embraced.

"The luck is running your way," said the man at Rowbotham's elbow. "I, on the other hand, have lost all my stake save this." And he tapped the table with the single forty-franc plaque. "Do you mind if I follow your bets?"

"Be my guest," responded Rowbotham.

"Thank you, monsieur," said Commissaire Darré, for it was he.

Rowbotham repeated his bets: maximum on black and thirteen. Darré followed him by placing his last forty francs—that's to say his Aunt Angélique's last forty francs—on black.

Black twenty-nine came up. Rowbotham was another ten thousand francs to the good, Darré a mere forty—but in fact it had been his first win of the day, having doggedly followed Lord Rosslyn's system and steadily lost since half past three.

"*Messieurs, faites vos jeux!*"

Rowbotham repeated his bets. Darré followed him with forty on black and forty on thirteen.

"*Les jeux sont faits, rien ne va plus,*" intoned the croupier in the flat, bored voice that they who preside over the fates of winners and losers have.

Somewhere beyond the trip-hammer that was belabouring the back of his head, Rowbotham was suddenly aware, when he woke up, that something—not too heavy or onerous, and sweetly scented—was leaning upon his left shoulder. Opening his eyes, he saw that it was a girl whose long black hair was trailing across his shirt-front. Two more degrees above the primeval ooze from which he was slowly rising and he remembered her name: Annabel. And then he remembered that he was in love with her, and she with him.

Someone was snoring across the room. Focussing, he saw a stocky character who bore some resemblance to Oliver Hardy (of Laurel and Hardy fame) asleep on the sofa opposite, his neatly button-booted feet perched on the armrest.

Swivelling his eyes, he took in a table set with stark white napery, brilliant silver, a vase of nodding carnations, the detritus of a meal and empty bottles of champagne to the number of four, no less. Then he remembered that he had helped to eat—and drink—that meal.

Carefully, lovingly detaching Annabel's head from his shoulder and laying it back against a pillow, he stalked out to the bathroom to relieve his bladder. Uncle Luigi—formerly Beppo in the annals of life—was in his usual place, face turned to the wall.

He was presently joined by the Oliver Hardy character.

"It has been a great night, *mon vieux,*" said Darré, for it was he.

"A great night," repeated Rowbotham, rinsing his hands, putting out his tongue, inspecting it in the mirror above the wash-basin and wincing at what he saw. "I must say it was frightfully decent of you to offer the wine tonight, Paul." They had slipped into first-name terms around about eight o'clock of that memorable evening, shortly before the *chef de partie,* the principal croupier, had announced that, the table having run out of funds, the bank was technically broken.

"Ernest," responded the other. "I will not say, nor labour upon, what you have saved me from. You have won half a million francs. I have done not badly. The champagne was an expression of my thanks."

"By Jove we were lucky," said Rowbotham.

"You can not imagine how lucky unless you were a regular player," declared the other. "For black to come up eleven times out of thirteen, and for thirteen to come up five out of thirteen times *en plein*—that must surely be written into the archives of the Monte Carlo Casino. Why, Ernest, your name will be remembered along with that of your illustrious compatriot, Mr. Charles Deville Wells."

"And who is he, Paul?" enquired the other.

"Who *is* he? *Ma foi*—C. D. Wells was the original Man Who Broke the Bank at Monte Carlo, my friend. Of whom the famous song was written.

They were both singing the chorus the second time when Annabel came in.

> "As I walk along in the Bois de Boulogne with an independent air,
> You can hear the girls declare, he must be a millionaire..."

She good-humouredly shooed them out of the bathroom, and they retired to the sitting-room and poured themselves a stiff cognac apiece. It was two o'clock in the morning they discovered.

"Miss Annabel, she's a considerable lady, that one," observed Darré. "You are a lucky fellow, my friend."

"She certainly has bloomed and blossomed most astonishingly since she's been in Monte Carlo," said Rowbotham.

"My friend, the air of Monte Carlo, the surroundings, are conducive to enriching a woman's beauty," said Darré. "The story of Monte Carlo is in large part the story of beautiful women who have graced her. I remember well my father telling me a tale (he was Commissaire of Police before me) of the two great beauties Liane de Pougy and La Belle Otero, both rivals, both heavy gamblers, both possessing fabulous jewellery that they certainly had not gained from doing charitable works among the poor. One night, La Belle Otero came into the Casino in scandalous *décolletage*, wearing pearls and diamonds valued at three million francs and more. Her rival Liane, who had heard beforehand that Otero was planning to make a spectacle, arrived in a virginal white dress with a single diamond suspended round her neck. But—and here is the cream of the jest—she had her maid following after her with all the rest of her jewels laid out on a velvet cushion."

"How priceless!" said Rowbotham. They both laughed uproariously and choked on their drinks.

"There is an alternative version of this tale," said Darré at length. "That the maid was not carrying the jewellery, but wearing it. In addition, there is an account that it was not the maid who bore the jewels but Liane's poodle dog."

They fell about, and were still falling, when Annabel came back into the sitting-room. She was immaculate from the crown of her sleek, sable head to the toes of her dainty shoes. One would not have thought that she had partaken in the winning of half a million francs, followed by a gourmet dinner *à trois* and four bottles of champagne. She looked, thought Rowbotham, as if she had just stepped out of a bandbox.

"Gentlemen," she said, "I think we have to address ourselves to the disposal of Uncle Luigi. I perceive that he is—although still faintly—beginning to make his presence known by other than sight on this hot night."

Commissaire Paul Darré, who by this time had been thoroughly filled in on the Uncle Luigi situation, gave the answer: "Permit me, mam'selle. I have an idea! And it has a certain interior elegance."

Along the coast road from Monte Carlo, through Menton, into Italy and on to the iridescent glories of the Gulf of Genoa, Luigi Gaudi drove at maximum speed, as if he were on the Monte Carlo race circuit. Liza watched him, watched his darkly pelted hands shifting the gear-stick by the faint light of the dashboard. They did not speak. She was alien to what they had set out to do together, having succumbed, merely, to the impulse of what was between them, what had been between them, what had been lost, what—possibly—might be regained.

Five miles short of Albenga, rounding a sharp bend, Luigi, who had taken a very good line through it, met head-on with a car coming the other way which, also being driven fast through the night, had not. The hired Mercedes containing Luigi and Liza performed a double somersault and ended up in a river bed. The former and putative future lovers died upon the instant, together. Oddly, the occupants of the other car escaped without a scratch.

The uncut diamonds, in their faulty sack, were spilled out of the riven car into the water. All save one, that one as big as a duck's egg.

It was picked up by a passing farmer some time later, when Luigi and Liza were both occupying unmarked graves in the nearby village cemetery and been forgotten. He found it on the river bank and used it as a paperweight for many years after, till it got lost.

They came to a dark cape beyond Cap d'Ail, a part of the coast that Darré knew well, because, as he explained, he and his father, the previous Commissaire of Police, had used to go fishing there from a little dory that they had used to row in all seasons, and the fickle Mediterranean being what it is (not by any means always the deep blue calm of the holiday posters; indeed, one of the most treacherous seas in the world), they fished at some risk. And this particular cape, said Darré, off this particular headland, right under the towering cliff, was the most profound deep in all the Riviera coast.

They came before dawn; left Charles and the limousine at the roadside and pushed Uncle Luigi—formerly known as Beppo Mazzini, a gentle man with simple and uncomplicated yearnings that had only been fulfilled through the manner of his own sacrifice—to the edge of the cliff. Commissaire Paul Darré went with them, but stayed a bit apart at the end, and took off his hat.

"So long, Uncle Luigi," said Ernest Rowbotham, by way of obsequies. "I've greatly enjoyed knowing you. We had fun.

The party's over now. You'll rest in the blue Mediterranean, where you sprang from. That's the best I can do.

"Good bye, Uncle."

He tipped the chair over the edge. The mummified figure, strapped to it, described with it many turns and convolutions before it whitely struck the dark water. Then Rowbotham and Annabel joined hands and went back to join Darré, the drive back to Monte Carlo, the Blue Train and the rest of their lives together.

Michael Butterworth lives in Bath, England, with his wife and children. He has gained a growing and enthusiastic following for his masterful suspense novels, which include *The Man in the Sopwith Camel* and *X Marks the Spot.*